THE CATS CALL ON
MELBA FOR HELP

Melba was standing hesitantly in the open drug store doorway, when up from behind the soda fountain counter popped Miss Toonie like a fuzzy piece of toast, and up with her sprang one-eyed Butch and about twenty other cats. Twenty more leapt suddenly from behind the candy rack, and then another thirty peeped out from thirty other hiding places around the store.

"Well!" shrilled Miss Toonie. "It's about time you got here!"

"But how did you know I was coming?" asked surprised Melba.

"What on earth do you mean?" squawked Miss Toonie. "We knew you were coming because of the plan. And what is it, by the way? We're all dying to know how you're going to save us."

At this, the cats moved in from all directions to surround Melba. Some rested on her feet; others crowded onto the counter near her elbows. One hundred and ninety-nine cat eyes looked expectantly at her, and Miss Toonie's cat face stared out from the middle of them.

Then an idea came to Melba. A sort of crazy plan it was, but she couldn't be choosy at a time like this.

The Dancing Cats of Applesap

By Janet Taylor Lisle

Illustrated by Joelle Shefts

BANTAM BOOKS
TORONTO · NEW YORK · LONDON · SYDNEY · AUCKLAND

This low-priced Bantam Book
contains the complete text of the
original hard-cover edition.
NOT ONE WORD HAS BEEN OMITTED.

RL 5, 009–012

THE DANCING CATS OF APPLESAP
A Bantam Book / published by arrangement with Bradbury Press, Inc.

Bantam Skylark edition / December 1985

Skylark Books is a registered trademark of Bantam Books, Inc.
Registered in U.S. Patent and Trademark Office and elsewhere.

ISBN 0-553-15348-X

Published simultaneously in the United States and Canada

Bantam Books are published by Bantam Books, Inc. Its trademark, consisting of the
words "Bantam Books" and the portrayal of a rooster, is Registered in U.S. Patent
and Trademark Office and in other countries. Marca Registrada. Bantam Books,
Inc., 666 Fifth Avenue, New York, New York 10103.

PRINTED IN THE UNITED STATES OF AMERICA

O · 0 9 8 7 6 5 4 3 2 1

The Dancing Cats
of Applesap

"You tell the story," says Melba Morris, sitting down in a living room chair by the Morris family telephone.

"No. You tell it," say I, a friend of the Morris family, more or less, and otherwise not someone who was involved. "If I tell the story, you'll just end up interrupting me all the time," I point out. "You're the one who's in it."

"You tell it anyway," answers Melba. "I'm not very good at telling stories in front of people. You start and I'll listen. I promise."

"Well, all right," I say. "I guess I've heard enough about those cats by now to begin, anyhow. How about this?

"Once upon a time there was a girl who . . ."

"Not that way!" interrupts Melba immediately.

"See?" I say, somewhat resentfully. "There you go interrupting."

"But you've got to tell people how to get here first!" exclaims Melba. "Tell them what I always say whenever anyone asks me how to get to Applesap, New York."

"Okay. Okay." I prepare to start off again.

But I know I won't get far with Melba sitting over there waiting to catch me up. Not that I mind, really. The best stories are built that way. One person starts talking and then another person decides that something was left out and has to speak up and change things. Then another person says: "No! It happened like this." And so, slowly, the story gets beaten into shape.

I guess this story is going to be that sort, with Melba doing the beating into shape.

"Right," says Melba from her chair. "Now go on and start telling. Don't pay any attention to me. I've got a phone call to make."

Chapter

—1—

WHENEVER ANYONE ASKS MELBA MORRIS WHERE Applesap, New York, is, this is what she says:

"If you've got a pin, it's easy. Have you got one? A thumbtack is okay too. My brother, Victor, did it once with a jackknife from all the way across the kitchen. He's a wild man. See, all you do is take your pin, or thumbtack or jackknife, squint your eyes a little, and stick it, pow, in the very middle of the map of New York State. That's where Applesap is, right at dead center. You can't miss it."

Applesap is the town where Melba Morris

lives. Lately, plenty of people have been asking for it. Word has got out about the pin too. Now folks from Tennessee and Nebraska and Texas and all over everywhere are sticking pins in and finding out how to get there.

Why, just last week a family came all the way from Alaska.

("California!" Melba interrupts. "They were from California.")

Well then, California. Just last week, a family came all the way from California. Melba was proud of that. She had a right to be proud. It wasn't so long ago that nobody ever asked where Applesap was. Nobody knew there was an Applesap to ask for, and even if they had known, they wouldn't have cared.

Applesap is the kind of small town that is all right if you live smack in it, but otherwise doesn't amount to very much. It isn't the capitol of anything. No presidents or beauty queens were ever born there. The only theater in town plays old Walt Disney movies that change about twice a year.

Applesap is a quiet town, a shy town, a town that feels its smallness and doesn't like to speak up because there are so many bigger and louder towns around. When there is a shopping mall up for grabs, or a roller rink, something big like that, it gets built in Glowville to the north or in Hopsburg to the south. They've got weight and throw it around. Applesap has a couple of schools, a library, a grocery store, a ladies' dress shop, and two drug stores . . . Not what you would call weight in this day and age.

Recently, though, there has been a run on Applesap. More people, tourist types, come by in one weekend than used to pass through in an entire year.

"And they're not coming all this way to get hot fudge sundaes at the Super Queen Drugs," Melba pipes up from her chair across the room. "No, sir. They're coming straight to Jiggs' Drug Store. Why, we're killing the Super Queen these days. I heard the owners are thinking of selling out and moving to Glowville where the competition isn't so rough.

"Miss Toonie's dancing cats are the main attraction, of course. There was a lady here yesterday from Hartford, Connecticut, who said those cats ought to be in the *Guinness Book of World Records*. And that we (that's

Miss Toonie, Mr. Jiggs, and I) ought to be in, too, for getting the act in shape.

"I thought that was a good idea, so I'm calling up the Guinness place this very morning. That's why I'm on the phone. I do things like that all the time now."

Melba Morris is ten years old, and she used to be just as shy and small and afraid to speak up as Applesap itself. At school, she was the one in the thick tortoise-shell glasses sitting farthest back from the teacher. On the playground, you would see her off by herself poking sticks through the fence or something equally dumb. She didn't like to walk up and say hello to anybody, even someone smaller than she was.

Melba looked at her feet a lot, and rubbed her skinny elbow a lot, and if anyone, by mistake, said hello to her, she would run to the ladies' room to polish her glasses. All her life she had been that way. It could have come from having an older brother who was a wild man.

Some people say if there is one child in a family who talks big and shows off and keeps a party jumping, there is bound to be another one who does the opposite. Maybe Melba was

the opposite one, or maybe she was born shy and would have been shy no matter what. It's hard to say. In any case, most kids hardly knew she existed, even the kids in her class at Applesap Elementary School.

Melba didn't complain. She said she liked being alone. She said she liked being ignored and didn't mind in the least that she was the only girl in the class who didn't get invited to Irma Herring's Easter party.

"It's okay," Melba told her mother. "I don't like Irma Herring anyway."

Even when it turned out that she had been invited, but that the invitation had somehow gotten lost in the mail, Melba said she would rather not go.

"Why not?" said Melba's mother. "Maybe if you went those children would get to know you better."

"Everybody has a streak of shyness in them," Melba's father said. "Everybody finds it hard to get to know people."

Melba shook her head. She went up to her room and closed the door.

In those days, Melba spent a good deal of time in her room. Heaven knows what she did in there. Perhaps she read books—exciting adventures of ancient princesses or of children marooned on desert islands.

("No, I didn't," interrupts Melba. "I didn't like stories. Nobody I know of was ever marooned on a desert island.")

Maybe she built scale models of rocket ships and blasted them out her window.

("Absolutely not," she declares. "Victor would have done something like that.")

Well, then perhaps she was teaching herself to knit. But whatever it was, she was doing a lot of it in her room. The only other place she ever went was to Jiggs' Drug Store, which, under normal circumstances, wouldn't have gotten her very far. Under normal circumstances she might have kept on going to Jiggs' and kept on being as shy as Applesap, New York, until both of them turned into dust. But, of course, circumstances at Jiggs' were not normal.

"They sure weren't," says Melba now, sitting down to make her phone call to the *Guinness Book*. "Jiggs' Drug Store didn't look like much on the surface, I know. But underneath, it had potential. And by the way," she adds, "I was *not* knitting in my room. I was thinking."

Chapter

—2—

JIGGS' DRUG STORE IS LOCATED AROUND THE
corner from the elementary school, on Dunn
Street. No one in those days before the dancing cats would have guessed it had potential.
When Melba started going there, it was a run-
down place and people didn't much go into
it anymore.

On rainy days at Jiggs' the roof leaked into
buckets set out on the floor. And on sunny
days the air turned hot and buggy. And on
any day the candy was stale. Furthermore,
there were the cats. Not one or two cats curled
up in out-of-the-way corners. Not even five

or six scampering after a ball of string. No. Jiggs' had cats in the worst possible way: all over everything by the dozen.

They slept in piles, dangling their tails down the cosmetic cases. They prowled in droves around the bottoms of the cigar and candy racks. They licked their nails on top of the comic books and cleaned their ears behind the cash register. Whenever a customer came into the store, cat faces looked out from every crook and cranny to see who it was. And cat eyes blinked and stared. And a hundred cat tails twitched. It was unnerving, to say the least.

Most children who wanted a soda or a candy bar after school went over to the Super Queen Drugs two streets down. The Super Queen was new, and fresh, and didn't have any cats at all. The Super Queen had two spotless, curving counters, flanked by rows of comfortable stools. It was the best place in town to meet up with people, and that, of course, was why Melba started going to Jiggs', where she could order a hot fudge sundae without having to polish her glasses all the time.

Jiggs' had only four battered chrome

ecream - candy - soda

JIGGS' DRUGSTORE

stools, and flies. They stuck onto the counter where Miss Toonie hadn't sponged off. Miss Toonie was the dried-up old scrap of a lady who ran the soda fountain. She had worked in Jiggs' for years and looked half cat herself.

Miss Toonie's mouth was edged with whiskers. Her hair fuzzed up the slope of her forehead like fur. On top of this, she was extremely ill-tempered. You couldn't say two words to Miss Toonie without getting your head snapped off. She was a grouch, everybody in town said so, and all on account of some man who had asked her to marry him forty years ago and then had run off and left her flat-footed, without even an engagement ring to show for it.

After that, Miss Toonie wouldn't have anything to do with men. Eventually, she put women on her blacklist too. Children, being the natural result of both men and women, made her cross just to look at. The only creatures Miss Toonie could stand were cats, and that is why so many had come to live at Jiggs' Drug Store.

They were a beat-up, cringing crowd, every one of which she'd found out on the Applesap streets. From the brink of starvation she had nursed them back to health, or from half freezing to death, or from mutilation by cars. Every monstrous thing that had ever been done to a cat had been done to the cats in Jiggs' Drug Store, and this made Miss Toonie crosser than ever.

"Cast out upon the world by people who call themselves human beings!" Melba heard her growl more than once under her breath.

Miss Toonie was so furious at the way the world was treating cats that by the time Melba started going to Jiggs' she wasn't talking to anyone, especially not to Mr. Jiggs, owner of the store and a sad specimen in his own right.

"Spineless," Miss Toonie called him, although privately Melba considered this a bit harsh. For once, as everyone in town knew, he had been a bright young man with dreams of running a bright and profitable business. Once he'd had hopes of expanding into branch stores in Glowville and Hopsburg, and of being named "Druggist of the Year" by the grateful citizens of New York State.

But, after all, Mr. Jiggs knew as little about expanding and growing up big as the soft-spoken town in which he had chosen to set up shop. He gave discounts when he should have charged double, and showed no talent for bill collecting, and he could not keep the account books straight. Even at the height of the store's popularity, twenty years ago, he was unable to make enough money to keep up with the modern trends.

So, when the Super Queen came to town, clean and businesslike and up-to-date, Mr. Jiggs was in no position to put up a fight. Gradually, customers who had been loyal to Jiggs' for years began doing their business at the Super Queen. And gradually, Mr. Jiggs, seeing his store wither, withered along with it until he became almost invisible.

Day after day he lurked in the shop's back room, strumming, for lack of anything better to do, an old guitar left to him by a musical aunt. His mournful chords grated on Miss Toonie's nerves.

"He's got no gumption and never did have," she complained to Melba, when they had become warily acquainted. "And lately he's turned mean. That's what comes of sitting around talking to yourself all day!"

Melba knew about Mr. Jiggs' meanness. He showed himself rarely, but when he did come forth—a small, balding old man with crumpled yellow skin—he did it in a rage.

His fists pounding the air, he shouted at Miss Toonie for not sponging off, and at the cats for being everywhere underfoot, and at the rain for dripping through the roof. When he shouted, his yellow skin turned a terrifying purple and his eyes bulged like marbles. But after he'd shouted, he went away again into the back room and took up his guitar and strummed his long, sad chords.

"We don't pay any attention to him," whispered Miss Toonie after he'd gone. This was true. A minute later, even the most nervous and beaten-up cats were curled up snoring, and Miss Toonie was sunk deep in a movie magazine, and the rain dripped as hard as ever into the buckets.

Only Melba sat frozen on her stool, her eyes wobbling a little behind her thick, glassy lenses.

Chapter

—3—

MISS TOONIE DISLIKED CHILDREN, BUT, ALMOST
from the first day, she found she didn't dis-
like Melba quite as much as the others.

Shy as the most timid kitten, Melba came,
at first once a week, then twice, and then almost every day after school. She always ordered the same thing: a hot fudge sundae.
Melba didn't make a fuss if the whipped
cream came out like a noodle. She didn't examine her spoon to see that it was clean. She
didn't talk much and she was neat, so Miss
Toonie didn't have to sponge off after her.

Melba gave Miss Toonie someone besides

the cats to complain to. And, on her side, Melba didn't mind listening. She was a good listener, even if her throat clamped shut when she tried to say something back. Luckily, Miss Toonie wasn't interested in answers.

"The rudeness of that man goes beyond understanding!" Miss Toonie would complain, but softly so her voice wouldn't carry into the back room. She didn't like to admit it, but she was a bit frightened of Mr. Jiggs herself.

"Never a pleasant word. Never a good morning or good night. And when I offer a suggestion for improving this miserable store he tells me to mind my own business! Well! And what is my business if it isn't this store?

"You be careful of him," she warned Melba. "He's a sick man. He doesn't have natural feelings for people. Sometimes," and here she would lower her voice further, "sometimes I think he beats the cats at night, after I've gone home. I've got no proof, of course, but they are often edgy and stirred up when I come back in the morning!"

Melba was afraid of Mr. Jiggs. She was afraid of Miss Toonie too, so bitter and fierce. But she was more afraid of meeting up with

Irma Herring and her sneering crowd coming home from school.

"Hey, rabbit!" they would call if they saw her across the street. And Melba, of course, would bolt just like a rabbit. "Hey, owl face! Where are you going? Hey, blind-as-a-bat!"

So Melba sat around Jiggs' Drug Store for thirty minutes, forty minutes, sometimes an hour. She nibbled her hot fudge sundae and waited for the Super Queen crowd to pass by on their way home. Even after their noisy, high-spirited groups had gone she stayed, licking her spoon and stroking the gnarled backs of nearby cats. She came to know a few friendly cats well, and the way those few perked up and ran over to say hello whenever she entered the store made Melba smile.

Not all the cats liked to be touched, she found. Some hissed and jumped away when she put out a hand. Some cringed in terror. Butch was a cringer. He was a large, gray alley cat of no particular distinction except that he had lost a front leg in a tragic street accident that had also bashed in the whole left side of his face. Through a single, evil-looking slit, Butch eyed the world, and more than one customer had fled the store, to Miss Toonie's delight, when confronted by his horrible stare.

But Butch was a sweet old fellow underneath, who would not think of raising a paw against anyone. Miss Toonie had found him crushed and lifeless on the store's front steps when she came to work one morning. Over many months she nursed him, and taught him in the bargain to eat the bright red cherries that decorated the tops of her sundaes. He adored them, and would take them only from her hand. When Melba offered him a cherry, Butch went into agonies of indecision. Shyly he edged toward her, limping awkwardly on his three legs. Still more shyly he waited, with lowered head, for her to make the first move. But when Melba reached out he flinched and trembled as if he thought she was about to hit him.

"He doesn't trust me," Melba said once, half to herself.

"And why should he?" snapped Miss Toonie, who had been watching suspiciously out of the corner of her eye. "For all he knows you might have been driving the truck that ran him down!"

One rainy day, Mr. Jiggs launched himself upon a tirade to end all tirades. He thundered and quivered with rage over the leaks, and tripped and swore over the cats, and he threatened to fire Miss Toonie "lock, stock, and barrel" if she didn't start sponging off "this very minute!" Then, warming up to the sound of his own voice, he turned on Melba, who was not doing a thing but biting her spoon a little too hard from nervousness.

"I know your type!" bellowed Mr. Jiggs at her terrified face. "Hanging around all day taking up space! If I catch you reading my comic books without paying for them I'll throw you out personally before you know what's hit!"

Miss Toonie laughed gaily after he'd stamped away.

"Well!" she said. "That was the worst fit in years. Something more than usual is bothering him I'd say!"

Melba was shaking with fear. She looked pleadingly at Miss Toonie.

"I didn't mean to take up space," she whispered, finding her voice somehow.

"Good heavens!" snorted the old lady. "Don't pay any attention to him. He's batty. Look at the cats. They're not the least worried." Not only were the cats not worried, but several dozen of them had quietly followed Mr. Jiggs into the back room. There, if Melba and Miss Toonie could have seen, they curled up peacefully on the floor surrounding his chair. And when, after throwing himself morosely down, Mr. Jiggs picked up his guitar to play again, cat ears all over the store stood up and quivered ecstatically with the first chord.

Melba was silent for a minute. Then she swallowed hard and spoke up again.

"Why doesn't Mr. Jiggs fix the leaks if they bother him so much?" she whispered. "Why does he allow the cats to live here?"

Miss Toonie shrugged. "I don't ask," she said. "Who can tell what goes on in the mind of such a man. I guess most of the time he's too sunk down to notice what happens in this store. And that's a good thing too, or my cats would probably be dead by now."

Melba nodded.

"There's only so much room in the world for small, helpless things like cats," Miss Toonie went on. "My cats are the leftovers, the ones who have gotten pushed out. This store is the last hope they have!"

"How many cats do live here?" asked Melba, feeling a little better.

"Round about a hundred last count," said Miss Toonie. "They come and go, you know, depending on what's for dinner."

"What is for dinner usually?"

"Old ice cream, old danish, old candy bars, that sort of thing. The mouse population isn't what it used to be around here."

"I guess not," said Melba.

She took a bite of hot fudge. "Where do they sleep?"

"Well, where do you think?" snapped Miss Toonie, suddenly tired of the discussion. "I can't take them all home with me, can I?"

Melba blushed and fumbled with her glasses. She finished her hot fudge sundae in silence, and got up to go. But Miss Toonie had been watching her. Leaning abruptly across the counter, she barked out:

"Why *do* you hang around here all the time? Haven't you got any friends or brothers or sisters?"

"Only one brother," answered Melba, with downcast eyes. "Five years older than I am."

"Well . . . ?" Miss Toonie's cat-fur eyebrows reared suspiciously.

"And. Well. He's crazy," muttered Melba. "One look at these cats and he'd go after his shotgun. He likes to shoot things."

Miss Toonie frowned. "Let him try," she snarled. "My cats would tear him to pieces!"

The old woman leaned backward and placed two dried-up paws on her hips.

"I stand by my cats!" she declared with unexpected fury. "The whole rest of my family was dead and buried long ago!"

"Sorry to hear it," murmured Melba, politely. Miss Toonie glared at her.

"I'd take cats over people any time," she said proudly. "They're clean. They're honest. And they don't play games. If they want to be friends they say so, and if they don't they stay away. You always know where you are with a cat!"

Miss Toonie spoke with such an accusing tone in her voice that Melba looked guiltily at her feet. Then she swallowed a huge gulp of air, gathered her courage, and spoke.

"Miss Toonie," she said, as straight as she could with her eyes still glued to her shoes. "Miss Toonie, I think you make the best hot fudge sundaes in the whole state of New York."

But Miss Toonie had turned her back. Frowning even more fiercely, she stuck a movie magazine up in front of her face and refused to say another word. She was a grumpy old lady all right, and why Melba should want to spend perfectly good time sitting around with her in a run-down, cat-ridden drug store is something most people wouldn't understand.

"Hey! Wait a minute!"

There goes Melba, interrupting again. Her hand is still set and ready on the telephone to dial up the *Guinness Book of World Records*.

"Hold up!" she says, holding up a free hand. "That's a pretty black picture you just painted of me and Miss Toonie, and I've got to say something about it. You've got me gulping and cringing like a two year old lost in the supermarket. (I will *not* be called a scared rabbit!) And you've made a bad mistake about Miss Toonie.

"Well, maybe she was a little grumpy, but it wasn't because of a man who ran off and left her. That's a groundless rumor that started up because people in Applesap couldn't think of any other reason why Miss Toonie was living alone.

"Whenever you see a woman who has decided to make her own way in life, immediately you find a whole lot of people who will tell you she's frustrated in love. It doesn't matter if it's not true. They'll whisper it around anyway, and speculate about what happened.

"See, people have got to talk, and one of

the best subjects to talk about is other people. And, if you can talk about other people so they end up sounding worse than you are, that's the best of all because it raises you up in the world. (I notice these things.)

"If Miss Toonie was grumpy, I guess I can see one reason why. There was all of Applesap whispering and snickering when the only thing she'd done was decide she was happier getting on by herself. I would have been angry too.

"In fact, that's my next point. All this cringing and gulping you have me doing doesn't get to the root of the matter. I was shy back then all right. But underneath, when no one was looking, I got angry as much as any person. You should have seen how fierce I used to get up in my room. I would stamp around and tell people off to their faces. I must have pinched Irma Herring five hundred times for not inviting me to her party. I was always pinching Irma, even before the party came up. I had a good reason.

"She and her friends used to laugh at me in class when I couldn't answer a question. She told everyone I was stupid. But one day, she figured a number problem wrong on the blackboard. It was my turn up next. I did it right, in front of everyone!

"That made Irma furious. When I walked back to my desk, she reached out and pinched me. Hard. Then all her friends laughed as if she'd done something smart. I felt terrible.

"After that, I was afraid of Irma. But underneath, I was angry. When I found out she'd invited everyone except me to her party, I was even more afraid, and more angry. I had such terrible feelings about Irma Herring's party that when the invitation did come, I didn't want to go.

"I didn't like parties back then anyway. There is nothing like a party for making a shy person stick out like a sore thumb. Everyone else is talking and running around together. And there is the shy person, over in a corner, getting ignored and being afraid people will notice how ignored she is.

"Anyway, just so you know I wasn't a cringer and a gulper all the way through, let me tell you that I did go to Irma's party in the end. But not in her house. I went in my own room where no one else could see. I talked and ran around and was the star of the whole party, just the way Victor always is. And when it came time to leave, I pinched Irma harder than ever, and stamped off down the street.

"Maybe it sounds dumb to pretend things like that in your room. But it wasn't such a bad way to operate. I was getting practiced up, and when the real day came . . .

"Well!" says Melba, cutting herself off. "That comes in later. I don't mean to jump the gun. And now, could you talk a little more quietly while I make this phone call? No, I'm not nervous. Not at all. I just need some quiet."

Chapter

—4—

MELBA'S SPEAKING UP IN FAVOR OF MISS Toonie's hot fudge sundaes changed things at the store.

In the days that followed, Miss Toonie wasn't quite so grumpy. Once in a while she let Melba take the cats for walks, a few at a time. And she taught her how to sort the new magazines and newspapers that were delivered in bundles to the store. She showed her how to make a hot fudge sundae, too, and how to twist the whipped cream can at such an angle—and release the button at the same time—that a dashing flourish of cream stood up straight on top, all ready to be crowned by the cherry.

Meanwhile, Melba was finding out that she didn't have to blush and gulp whenever she wanted to ask Miss Toonie a question. And she certainly didn't have to worry about talking to the cats, which she did a lot of.

In fact, those afternoons at the store became happier and happier and longer and longer until Melba was spending hardly any time thinking in her room. Melba's mother noticed.

"You've found a friend?" she asked hopefully.

"Well, sort of," answered Melba, who was not sure, even now, that Miss Toonie could be counted as a friend.

"It's that old grouch down at Jiggs' Drug Store," volunteered Victor, who had somehow found out. "Everybody else hates her."

"That's because nobody else knows her very well," said Melba stoutly, but then she blushed so hard that her mother had to tell Victor to hush up and let people make friends where they found them.

So Melba kept on going to Jiggs', and business being worse than usual there, she and Miss Toonie mostly had the place to themselves. Except for Mr. Jiggs, of course, whose face, if they had noticed it, was turning yellower and meaner by the hour. Miss Toonie was right. Something more than usual was bothering the old man. Now he had taken to pacing up and down the back room, startling the cats at his heels with sudden turns

and swerves. His tables were covered with open account books. Mr. Jiggs paced and figured and paced again. Finally, one dark morning while the cats looked on reproachfully, he brought his fist down in the middle of one particularly dilapidated book and stalked out to the soda fountain counter to announce the bad news.

"Closing down!" shrieked Miss Toonie. "But why?"

"Why do you think!" he roared. Then he disappeared into the back room again, took up his guitar, and struck dire chords.

In shock, Melba asked the same question that afternoon.

"But why? It's so nice here!" By then Miss Toonie had composed herself. She answered in her snappiest voice.

"Well! Why do you think? I suppose you think you've been supporting the store on your measly one sundae a day. Well! You haven't been! Jiggs has gone broke. He's selling out."

"But I thought you hated having customers in the store!" cried Melba.

Miss Toonie ignored her. "There's to be a

dry cleaning establishment taking over next week," she fumed. "Think of it! Right here where I'm standing now will be a rack of plastic-covered clothes whose only aim in life is to get picked up on time!"

Miss Toonie sniffed such a fierce, sad sniff that her whiskers stood up on end.

Melba stood up too, scattering cats. Her glasses slid sideways.

"You can't sell out," she pleaded in a scared voice. "Jiggs' Drug Store has always been here. What would people do without Jiggs'?"

"Don't talk to *me* about it," said Miss Toonie. "Talk to him!" She skewed her thumb in the direction of the back room. "And as for what people will do, well, they'll do what they do now, anyway. They'll go to the Super Queen. No one will even notice we've folded. You'll see."

"I'll notice!" exclaimed Melba, blushing horribly. "And what about the cats? You can't take them home with you, you said it yourself."

Miss Toonie looked at the counter.

"Very true," she agreed. "Poor cats. They will, I suppose, simply have to disperse."

"No, they won't! They won't go! These cats love you. They're your family, remember?"

"Cats are cats," said Miss Toonie with a brave wave of her hand. "They'll go. They'll go off to somebody else who can feed them." She groped for her handkerchief and made a last desperate effort to look fierce behind it.

Now Melba shut her lips, and looked down at a worn place under the counter where hundreds of thoughtless feet had scraped and gouged the brittle wood. Cats had been there, too. Fuzzy strands of cat fur were snagged on splinters.

"He can't do this to you!"

"He can do it," answered Miss Toonie. "It's his store."

"No, it isn't," said Melba, low and threatening as a cornered cat's growl. But her eyes were already filled up with tears. In a minute, she knew, she would have to run away to hide them. That made her angrier, because how many times can you pinch people like Irma Herring up in your room without realizing it doesn't prove a thing? They don't know the difference. They go on talking or eating dinner or whatever they are doing in real life and they don't feel the tiniest prick of outrage, not the lightest drop of a tear. They go on, thought Melba, turning her head to look, playing a guitar as if nothing terrible were happening at all.

Suddenly, Melba was running, but it wasn't out the front door. She was rounding the entrance into the back room, and even before she got there she was yelling at Mr. Jiggs.

"You spineless man!" she yelled, giving him, at last, a solid dose of his own medicine. "How can you sit here playing that guitar while our store goes down the drain? There are people who depend on this store and you're not even trying to save it. You don't even care!"

Then, before Mr. Jiggs, staggering up from his chair, could throw her out, shy Melba Morris stamped out of the store herself, right past Miss Toonie and all the cats, everybody staring.

Chapter
—5—

MELBA STAMPED DOWN THE SIDEWALK IN A fury. She stamped up Dunn Street and down School Street and along Orchard Street to where the Morris family lived in a house backed up to a middle-sized field. The more she thought about Jiggs' Drug Store closing down, and about the cats and poor Miss Toonie, and about herself without a drug store to her name, the angrier she became. She stamped into the house, pounded up the stairs to her room, and finding that unsatisfactory (too small for proper stamping), she stamped down again and out the back door.

Half of her, it must be said, was horrified by what she had done. To have shouted at Mr. Jiggs so loudly—"How rude," said a voice inside her. To be out stamping around in broad daylight—"Not the least like you," said the voice.

"Go hide yourself," the voice advised.

"Blush and look guilty," another voice whispered.

"You are sticking out like a sore thumb!" they hissed together. "What will people say? Quick! Shuffle and be shy."

Melba, however, was in the grip of a glorious anger which made stamping the most natural thing in the world, and shuffling completely impossible. So she stamped out the back door into the yard, and there, abruptly, came face to muzzle with her brother, Victor.

The muzzle was the barrel of his shotgun. Its black nose was pointed straight at her!

"Out of the way! You're in the line of fire!" screamed Victor, only just in time.

Melba lurched backward. The shotgun exploded with a terrible blast that echoed across the yard and through the open field beyond. A covey of quail leaped from a hiding place

in the tall grass to flap off at top speed. In the following silence came a soft rustle. A squirrel dropped out of a nearby bush, shot through.

"Got him!" screeched Victor. He raced across to grab the victim by its tail. Melba felt dizzy. She put her hands over her ringing ears and closed her eyes. Poor squirrel. It was very dead.

"Hey!" crowed Victor, running back to her. "Don't ever do that again!"

"Do what?" Melba opened her eyes, but tried not to look at the remains of the squirrel dangling from his hand.

"Jump out the door that way before anyone can see you. I almost blew your head off."

"I know," choked Melba. "I'm still shaking."

This seemed to please Victor. "Better get out of here now, too," he said manfully. "I'll be doing some more shooting, I guess. I've got some friends coming over soon. We're going after that groundhog in the field."

"Do you have to?" asked Melba weakly.

"Guess so. He's been at the garden."

Melba looked at her feet.

"Better get going," urged Victor, waving a bloody hand. Squirrel blood.

Melba went. She crept back up to her room and lay down on her bed. Her heart pounded. Her arms shook. She felt terrible. Jiggs' Drug Store was going out of business, and suddenly there wasn't a drop of anger left in her.

Melba puts the phone down with a bang. She leaps to her feet and walks in a fast circle around the living room. Then she sits down by the phone again and rubs her elbow. Maybe calling the *Guinness Book of World Records* isn't as easy as it sounds at first, even when you've figured out the area code and know the telephone number by heart.

"Oh, be quiet," says Melba. "I was just thinking about Victor. I got blown over pretty easily back then, by him and everybody else. It makes me mad to think how that shotgun blast knocked me out just when I was getting worked up enough about Jiggs' Drug Store to do something about it. All I could do instead was cry. I cried on my bed with my head under the pillow and all the time there were these blasts and pops going off in the background.

"That was Victor out in the field with his friends. They were shooting at the groundhog and a whole lot of innocent, terrified rabbits.

"The more I thought about those rabbits, the more I thought how Miss Toonie's cats would be out on the street soon, getting shot at and kicked around, with nobody to love them.

"I felt like one of those cats myself, sort of homeless and scared. Every time I closed my eyes I'd see Victor's shotgun pointed straight at me, and I'd run, in my mind, up a tree. But even trees aren't safe against shotguns. I guess I must have run around like that in my mind for about two hours trying to think of good places to hide. In the end, I fell asleep. But there was no place good enough to be completely safe."

Melba pauses, fiddling with the telephone cord.

"Do you have a copy of the *Guinness Book of World Records* around anywhere?" she asks, suddenly changing the subject. "I haven't read it lately. Maybe they already have a section on dancing cats. Living in a small town like Applesap, New York, I don't always hear about what's going on in the world.

"I was thinking: if those cats turned up here, they've probably turned up in other places too. A place like New York City has probably had smarter and fancier dancing cats for years. If that's true, I sure would look silly calling up the *Guinness Book* about a plain old thing that happens every day.

"I'm tired," says Melba, getting up again, but slowly this time. "I think I'll go outside and sit on the porch, if you'll excuse me. I need to be alone to think the problem out."

Chapter

—6—

VICTOR'S SHOTGUN BLAST CERTAINLY HAD knocked the stuffing out of Melba. In gloom, she stayed in her room most of the next day, which was Saturday. The sky had turned an evil gray during the night. Rain was falling. Out on the front porch lay the carcasses of five skinny rabbits. Melba tried not to look at them when she came down for breakfast.

Victor was out on the porch too, skinning a sixth and keeping an eye on the muddy vegetable garden that ran along the side of the house. Miraculously, the groundhog had escaped the shoot-out of the day before.

"I bet he thinks he's some smart hog," grumbled Victor.

"How do you know he's not a girl?" asked Melba from the kitchen.

It was still raining at four o'clock when Melba left her room again and came down to pick an umbrella out of the hall closet. There isn't much that's worse than sitting around a house that has a lot of dead rabbits lying just outside the front door.

Melba went out, by the back door. She didn't intend to go to Jiggs'. She intended never to look at that drug store again. But, in her misery, she splashed down Orchard Street, and plodded along School Street, and shuffled up Dunn Street until, almost by accident, she found herself standing in front of Jiggs' Drug Store.

It was closed. Outside, the rain had beaten the store's wooden shingles to a sodden black. Inside, all the lights were out. Melba edged up to the grimy window and peered through. Nothing was stirring. She tried the wooden door. It was locked.

No! It wasn't! The door opened. Melba was standing hesitantly in the open doorway, a little afraid of running into Mr. Jiggs, when up from behind the soda fountain counter popped Miss Toonie like a fuzzy piece of toast, and up with her sprang one-eyed Butch and about twenty other cats. Twenty more leapt suddenly from behind the candy rack and then another thirty at least peeped out from thirty other hiding places around the store.

"Well!" shrilled Miss Toonie, in her most ill-tempered voice. "It's about time you got here. We've been waiting for hours!"

"But how did you know I was coming?" asked surprised Melba, when she had been invited in and was sitting astride her usual stool.

"What on earth do you mean?" squawked Miss Toonie. "We knew you were coming because of the plan. And what is it, by the way? We're all dying to know how you're going to save us."

At this, the cats moved in from all directions to surround Melba. Some rested on her feet; others crowded onto the counter near her elbows. One hundred and ninety-nine cat eyes looked expectantly at her, and Miss Toonie's cat face stared out from the middle of them.

"What plan?" gasped Melba.

"Now that really is the limit!" howled Miss Toonie. "You go stamping around this store telling Mr. Jiggs he's a spineless worm (which he is, of course) for selling out without a fight, and then you go stamping off in a perfect fury. And now here you are back again with nothing to show for it at all. When people get angry they usually *do* something about it! I guess you're about as spineless as everyone else around here.

"Come along cats," said Miss Toonie, waving them off with an arm. "False alarm. Let's get packing. Jiggs wants the whole place in boxes by Monday morning sharp. That's when he signs the final sale papers," she added, turning to Melba. "He's over seeing the dry cleaners now to negotiate the price."

"Hey, wait a minute!" shouted Melba. "I didn't know I was supposed to make a plan!"

"Who else?" shrugged Miss Toonie. "You as good as said you would."

Melba blushed and gulped. Then, since they were slipping down anyway, she took off her glasses and began to polish them hard on a shirttail.

Chapter

—7—

"MAYBE YOU NEED SOME FOOD FOR THOUGHT," Miss Toonie said. "There is nothing like a hot fudge sundae for stirring up brain cells."

"No, thanks. I'm not hungry," said Melba. She was sitting on the stool doing her best to think straight and fast. It wasn't something she was very good at. Victor, of course, was the fast thinker in the family. With him around all the time, Melba hadn't gotten much practice on making plans over the years. She was used to standing about saying things like:

"What shall we do now, Victor?"

Or:

"Victor, are you sure it will work?"

Melba wished her brother were here to take over. He would have about ten plans ready in as many minutes, and being older, he could probably carry them out better.

"How about if I ask Victor? He'd know what to do," Melba asked Miss Toonie.

"Not on your life!" she squawked in alarm. "I'm not letting that gunslinger anywhere near my cats. The only plan he'd think of is how to get them out in some field for target practice."

"I guess you're right," admitted Melba. She pushed two cats out of her lap and put her elbows on the counter.

"I can see we're crowding you," said Miss Toonie. "Nobody can think with a bunch of cats breathing in her face. We'll take ourselves off to the back room and let you alone for a while. It's feeding time, anyhow."

"That's all right," said Melba, but Miss Toonie put two fingers in her mouth and blew a low, sharp whistle.

It was answered by a bustle from all corners, an unfurling of cat tails and a beat of cat paws marching across the room. Melba swiveled around on her stool to watch the exodus.

To her surprise, the cats did not come forth in a pushing, scampering jumble. Instead, they lined up, head to tail to head in the sort of queue you see in front of the movie theater on a first-run night.

How was this? Each cat seemed to know its exact place in the lineup. While some cats waited their turn, others dropped into line, one at a time, in what appeared to be a well-learned order. There was no hissing or scratching to get ahead. Quietly, as if it were the sort of thing cats did more naturally than any other, they took their places and stood at attention, their tails shot straight up in the air. Broken down, earless, and legless, they looked like a proud column of old soldiers about to set off down Main Street for the Memorial Day parade.

When the last cat was in place, the line went the length of the store. It ran out of space at the comic-book rack, sailed around and doubled back to the lipstick counter, and continued along to where the rubber gloves and shower caps were shelved. There it tapered off, and in silence each cat looked ahead through the tail of the one before it, waiting for some further signal.

It came, another low whistle from Miss Toonie. Forward surged the line into the back room, while Miss Toonie, bending at the waist, gave a fond rub to each back passing through.

When the last cat had passed, she turned proudly to Melba and, in keeping with the military air of the procession, dashed off a stern salute.

"Sorry for the delay," she said apologetically. "It doesn't do to have them herding about. Tears up the place and then old Jiggs is cross."

"But . . ." gasped Melba.

"Oh, the cats understand quite well," Miss Toonie went on. "They've run a tight ship from the beginning. I guess they figured out early on that order was the key to staying on in this store.

"You know, out on his own and singly, a cat doesn't appear to have much sense of order. People always complain that cats have minds of their own and lead stubborn, independent lives. And that's true. It's true for any animal that lives apart.

"But get a mass of smart animals together, whether it's elephants, ants, or cats, and you'll see how order gets set up right away. Everybody pitches in to make life more bearable for himself and everybody else. When you're living at close quarters, it's the only possible way of getting along."

"That's fantastic!" exclaimed Melba. "What else do they do besides march?"

"Nothing else that I know of," shrugged Miss Toonie, "and it's not so fantastic really. Look at the circus. It's got ponies and dogs and tigers walking about in lines all over the place. And doing a lot more besides."

"That's right," said Melba. "A lot more besides. You could work up an act with these cats and join the circus. Why haven't you done it?"

"The circus!" said Miss Toonie, scornfully. "My cats are not traveling performers! They're quiet, ordinary folk who want to live together in quiet, ordinary ways. It's not so much to ask, is it? A roof over one's head and a regular dinner hour?"

Miss Toonie took hold of her handkerchief and swabbed her nose violently.

"Now you sit there and think!" she barked at Melba. Then she swayed off tragically into the back room after the cats.

Melba sat on at the counter flicking dead flies to the floor in a dreamy way. As she sat, a smile spread over her face. Flick went a fly off the counter. Tick went a part of her brain.

Melba was launching the tenth or eleventh fly when the idea came. A sort of crazy idea it was, but she couldn't be choosy at a time like this.

"Miss Toonie!" yelled Melba. "Miss Toonie, come here!"

"It's funny," says Melba, reappearing suddenly from the front porch, "but when people expect you to do a thing, put their trust in you somehow, then suddenly, you begin to think maybe you *can* do it. And before you know it, even if you're shy as a groundhog, you find you have done it and that it wasn't very hard at all.

"For instance, I'm a little nervous right now, maybe you've noticed, about calling up the *Guinness Book of World Records*. They're a big outfit. They don't like to be bothered with nobodies from places like Applesap, New York. Maybe they'll laugh when they hear about the cats and tell me to go fly a kite. Maybe they'll hang up in my face. I'm nervous about it, but listen!

"Now that I've told you I'm going to do it, you kind of expect me to go through with it, right? And since you expect me to do it, I feel a little better about picking up the phone. You're on my side, backing me up, if you see what I mean.

"So, here goes. I'm really calling them, *right now!*"

Chapter
8

WHILE THE CATS FEASTED ON BLACK RASP-
berry ice cream and hot dogs ("Might as well
give them the works," sniffed Miss Toonie.
"Nobody else is going to buy this stuff
now."), the old lady listened to Melba's plan.
She blinked, and scratched her ear. Then she
shook her head.

"It'll never work," said Miss Toonie. "Better think of something else."

"Why wouldn't it work?" asked Melba.
"The cats would be doing the same thing they
do now, only out where people can see them."

"Listen," said Miss Toonie, waving off a

fly. "It's one thing to march around when dinner is waiting in the next room. Quite another to go parading along Main Street. My cats are afraid of that street, anyhow. They've got bad memories of being mowed down out there."

"We could pack a lunch," urged Melba. "They'd follow you if they knew you were carrying food."

"Can't say whether they would at all," grumbled Miss Toonie.

"We'd go tomorrow afternoon. It's Sunday and people aren't out driving around so much," said Melba, feeling, suddenly, a little like Victor. "Most people are hanging around their back yards wondering what to do next. Sunday is slack time in Applesap, just the time to draw attention to ourselves."

"Now see here," snapped Miss Toonie. "I'm not going to have my cats making fools of themselves to entertain a few nitwits lolling about after Sunday dinner. And what would happen after that? I don't see where it would lead."

"It would lead," said Melba, polishing her glasses with determination, "right back to the store. Don't you see, Miss Toonie? We need customers, and fast. Why we'll have every kid in town following the cats down the street, and every man and every woman close behind wondering what's going on. And when they get here they'll be meeting up with each other and milling around and talking about the cats. And that's when some of them will start wanting a coffee or a soda. And others will start remembering some little thing like pipe cleaners or shower caps that they need, and the next day more people . . ."

"And the Super Queen is closed on Sundays!" cut in Miss Toonie.

"That's right!" shouted Melba, just remembering.

"And in they'll come to get what they can't get anywhere else for once!" snickered Miss Toonie, showing her first healthy interest in customers in years.

"And just to celebrate Jiggs' staying open on Sundays," said Melba, as if it were always part of the plan, "you'll be serving free ice-cream cones!"

"Now, wait a minute," coughed Miss Toonie, pulling up short. "I've never in my life heard of Jiggs giving away free ice-cream cones. He's always been a straight businessman: no slick advertising, no come-on tricks, no free giveaways.

"Of course," she added slyly, "he needn't know what we're up to."

Miss Toonie shot a thoughtful look through the front windows, opened her mouth to say something else, and . . . suddenly closed it with a click.

"Hush down," she told Melba. "Jiggs is here. That's his car I see driving up." She made a dash toward the back room for the cats.

"I don't know what that man thinks," she called to Melba, "but he's never yet figured out it's his goods keeping these cats from starvation."

Hoot! went her low whistle, and in an instant the cats marched out in double time and their food trays were slung in the sink for washing. Then everyone fell into position in his usual pile or under his usual rack. By the time Mr. Jiggs arrived, small and yellow and toting a large brief case stuffed with final sale papers, Miss Toonie had her face in a movie magazine.

Mr. Jiggs shuffled gloomily through the store without a word. When he stooped to pick up his guitar from behind the drug counter, a hundred cat tails twitched and one hundred ninety-nine eyes watched the movement intently. Mr. Jiggs passed out of sight into the back room. Soon the store was filled with the sound of his long, sad strums again. All around Melba the cats, apparently satisfied that nothing unusual was afoot, were closing their eyes and resting their chins on their paws. A general purr arose, vibrating the air like the noise crickets make on a warm moonlit evening.

If Miss Toonie was irritated by Mr. Jiggs' strumming, the cats, Melba noticed, were soothed by it. They loved the music, clearly, and listening herself, Melba had to admit its beauty. The melodies were a little sad perhaps, but beautiful, as sad music is that comes straight from the heart.

"Pss-sst!" hissed Miss Toonie, interrupting the sleepy quiet. She beckoned Melba closer.

"We can't talk here," she whispered. "If I know old Jiggs (and after all these years I guess I know him), he's socked in for the evening with that instrument."

"I've got to go home anyway," said Melba

apologetically. "It's almost dinner time and my parents will be wondering where I am."

"Right!" said Miss Toonie. "I'll meet you back here at eight o'clock sharp tomorrow morning. We won't have to worry about Jiggs then. He spends his Sundays locked up in his house with the shades drawn."

"Why does he do that?" asked Melba getting down from her stool.

"Who knows," whispered the old lady. "He *used* to be a nice, regular fellow, a man who could hold his head up in town and feel proud of himself. Why he'd walk down the street and people would take their hats off to him and ask him for Sunday dinner and such." Miss Toonie shook her head.

"That was a long time ago, before the Super Queen came to town. Afterward, when business began to fall off, he went into hiding. I guess he couldn't face up to the folks who used to be his customers but had gone over to the Super Queen. He's still a proud man, that Jiggs," said Miss Toonie wistfully.

"But spineless!" she added with an ill-tempered snap, and she gazed fiercely at the cats, who lay about her like children in soft, sleepy piles. Then smoothing her skirt she came around the end of the counter to fetch her coat and hat. A minute later she was holding the door open for Melba, and the two went out into the rain, groping to raise their umbrellas against the wet and the trickle.

Chapter

——9——

MELBA WOKE UP THE NEXT MORNING (A FINE, blue, Sunday morning), and the first thing she did was have an attack of the jitters. This was nothing unusual. The jitters were as much a part of Melba's life as the weather. Like the weather, they came and went, blackening some days with dread, clouding up others with worry, blowing an hour to nervous pieces and then dying down and fading away again.

The jitters might attack three times in one week or three times in one day, or they might settle in for a sweaty-palmed siege. Often, they came at the worst possible moment: when Melba wanted to answer a teacher's question but then (the jitters!) couldn't open her mouth; when Melba tried out for the school play but then (gasp—the jitters!) could only choke and gurgle on stage.

Time after time the jitters froze Melba dead in her tracks and set her up to be laughed at, and whispered about, and finally swept impatiently aside.

After a while, Melba began to get the jitters by just thinking that she might get the jitters. That was worse, because it meant she couldn't do things that she wanted, secretly, very much to do. She couldn't take swimming lessons because she might get the jitters. She couldn't telephone people because she might freeze.

Melba couldn't even talk about the jitters or they might take revenge for being told on and fly down and grab her.

This fine, blue morning, the jitters had Melba by the throat and it didn't make a bit of difference that she knew where they came from. Idiotically, they came from a dream she'd had the night before.

The dream was about Irma Herring's

Easter party which Melba had somehow stumbled into the middle of, even though it was the last place on earth she wanted to be. (Dreams will do that to you every time.)

Irma was standing up very tall in a bright yellow party dress and she was shooting Victor's shotgun off into the air.

"Get the cats! Get the cats! Get the cats!" Irma was chanting. She shot the gun off in between chants. Melba was cowering in a corner. Suddenly she looked down and saw a terrible thing happening. Her body was changing into a cat body, all fur and paws and a hairy, white belly.

"Help!" screamed Melba in her dream, but the sound came out only as a shrill cat's mew.

Melba woke up, hot and clammy. She examined her stomach to make sure it wasn't a cat belly. Then she remembered the cat-march plan. That's when the jitters came down in a black swarm all over her. They made her stomach quake and her knees go limp and her throat wrench shut so that she could hardly breathe.

The plan all of a sudden became a terrible plan. It wouldn't work. It had Melba walking down Main Street like a fool with everybody staring at her. It had the cats causing a traffic jam and getting hauled off to jail. It had Miss Toonie screaming and shaking her fist at her for thinking up such a dumb idea.

Oh, dear, moaned Melba to herself. *Why did I ever do it?*

"I feel sick," she groaned aloud. "I'll have to stay right here in my room because I feel so terrible."

But Melba couldn't stay in her room. Irma Herring was there in her yellow party dress, and even though she was only left over from a dream, she scared Melba enough to send her out the door and downstairs for breakfast.

The only person in the kitchen was Victor. He was eating an enormous bowl of cereal, and from the way he was going through it Melba knew there was nothing holding him back from his day. Jitters weren't a subject that Victor knew anything about. As for dreams, if he had them at all, Melba thought they would be about Victor chasing things down rather than something chasing him.

This morning, Victor was intent on getting his groundhog, and you had to admire how he was going about it.

"Look at this!" he announced, when Melba sat down at the table. She poured herself about enough cereal to keep a mouse going for five minutes, and looked. Victor was drawing a map of the field on a pad of paper.

"See, the groundhog has got two holes that we know of. One is up in the corner by the fence. And the other, since he's no dummy of course, is right down opposite our vegetable garden," Victor explained. He marked the map with a black X.

"Now what we're going to do is split flanks, with half of us covering the fence and the other half hiding in those bushes near the garden. Then, at the signal—which I'll give, of course—the garden troops will make a lot of noise, just to let the groundhog know that the garden isn't the place where he can get his lunch today.

"So, naturally, after a while, he'll start poking his head out the other door. That's where I'll be with my shotgun, and *whammo!*—he won't know what hit him!"

"It's a good plan," Melba had to admit. "Think it will work?"

"It will work, all right. I'll make it work," said Victor. He leaned back in his chair, very pleased. Victor grinned. It was the same big, broad friendly grin that made everyone like him and want to be with him, crazy or not. Melba couldn't help smiling too. She poured herself another bit of cereal and leaned back in her chair the way Victor was leaning, cool and casual. Victor seemed to appreciate this.

"Hey!" he said. "Do you want to come along? We could use another person in the garden to make noise."

Melba shook her head. "I've got plans of

my own today," she answered, trying to sound businesslike. Victor sat up and eyed her.

"What plans?" he asked suspiciously, because Melba usually didn't have things like that. Melba usually waited for him to have plans.

"Oh, something."

"Something down at that dumb drug store, I bet," said Victor. He eyed her again. "Hey! You know what I heard?"

"What?"

"They're going out of business."

"No. They're not," said Melba.

"Yes, they are. Everybody at the Super Queen knows it. Everybody says it's about time, too. That old wreck of a place is an eyesore in this town, and the people who run it are eyesores too!"

"They are not!" cried Melba, blushing with anger. Victor smiled and shook his head at her.

"Listen," he said, lowering his voice. "Don't hang around there anymore. People see you there and they laugh. The place is a dump. Only losers go there. You don't want to be a loser, do you?"

"Yes!" cried Melba. "I mean, no!" She pushed away from the table in confusion, and stood. Victor was grinning up at her foolishly. He didn't know anything.

"What I mean is they are not losers," Melba said fiercely. "They are my friends!"

"Come on," whined Victor. "Stay here and help me today. It will be fun."

"Stay here and take orders from you, you mean!" called Melba over her shoulder. She was already running for the door. Then she was on the sidewalk heading for Jiggs' Drug Store with long, determined strides. And not until she actually saw that old building looming up over the sidewalk did she remember the jitters. But, by that time, they were somewhere down deep, hiding out quietly like the groundhog in the field.

"Hello? Is this the company that publishes the *Guinness Book of World Records?* It is? Oh, wow! I mean (*ahem*) my name is Melba Morris and I have, or I guess I have, well, maybe I have, a world record to report."

("That wasn't a very good beginning, was it," says Melba over her shoulder. "I should have sounded more forceful. They've put me on hold.")

"Hello? Oh, yes. I was just telling the other man . . . My name is Melba Morris and . . . What? Okay, I'll wait."

("They put me on hold again," explains Melba with her hand over the receiver. Her glasses are falling sideways, the way they do when she's nervous and her nose gets sweaty. "The switchboard is overloaded with calls. That's strange, isn't it? When you think of a world record you usually think of something that happens only once in a lifetime, or maybe once in twenty years. And here is the *Guinness Book* company clogged up with people calling in to report world records from all over the place.")

"Hello? Yes. This is . . . No! No, I'm Melba Morris from Applesap, New York, and it's about dancing cats, not swallowing nails. What? I didn't say prancing rats, it's *dancing cats* I'm reporting. Can't you send someone out to look at them? Everybody around here thinks they're fantastic. All right, I'll hold on."

("They thought I was somebody from Tulsa, Oklahoma who had swallowed twenty-five nails and lived through it," says Melba, wiping a clammy palm on her jeans. "What a dumb thing to do. I guess some people sit around thinking of crazy things to do just to get written up. I hope the Guinness people can see the difference between those kinds of records and our cats. Our cats aren't showing off. They're a plain miracle!")

"HELLO!" shouts Melba into the phone. "This is me. Melba. Isn't it my turn yet? I've been waiting for a long time! See, I've got these cats who . . . But I've *been* holding!"

(Melba rolls her eyes up to the ceiling the way Miss Toonie does when she wants to look exasperated. "*Whew!*" she says. "And to think that I was scared about making this phone call!")

Chapter
—10—

IF EVER THERE WAS A DAY FOR MARCHING down Main Street, it was that cool, blue, spring Sunday in Applesap, New York. Applesap may have been small. It may have lived timidly for most of the year in the shadows of those louder and pushier towns of Hopsburg and Glowville. But every once in a while a day would come, a fine, clear, promising day, to make Applesap stand up as proud and confident as any town in America.

On those days, people in Applesap walked with an extra lilt in their steps, and shop windows shone with an extra sparkle, and life

took on an air of importance. On this particular Sunday, for no reason that anyone could put a finger on, Applesap was practically bursting with sparkle.

Melba felt it as she walked along the sidewalk toward Jiggs' Drug Store. The sparkle straightened her shoulders and lifted her chin and finally pranced her incongruously across Main Street to Dunn, as if she were a majorette leading the band.

Fitting her old-fashioned key into the old-fashioned lock on the store's front door, Miss Toonie felt it, and sniffed the air suspiciously.

"If I didn't know better I'd say it was a wonderful day today," she muttered almost cheerfully to the cats who swarmed up to greet her.

Across town, the mayor of Applesap, biting into his breakfast egg, felt it and decided on the spot to construct a roller-rink pavilion to beat the devil out of Glowville's.

And all over town people were pushing up their windows and congratulating themselves on the greenness of their lawns. Churchgoers were skipping up the steps to their churches. Paperboys were hurling their papers like javelins. Dogs galloped at the heels of their rabbits, and even groundhogs (especially Victor's, soggy and hungry after two days of underground hiding) nosed up from their holes for a quick gulp of that glittering air.

Meanwhile, as Melba bounded up behind Miss Toonie to enter Jiggs' Drug Store, Jiggs himself, in his dark house at the edge of town, twitched up a shade and peeped out for exactly three seconds before sadly closing it back down again.

"Spineless worm," snapped Miss Toonie to Melba. "Just look how he made himself dinner on my counter last night and didn't even have the politeness to sponge off after."

"He's left his guitar here, too," said Melba. She picked it up from the counter's far end, where about twenty cats had been using it for a pillow.

"And look," she added. "A string is broken."

"Don't tell me to look," growled Miss Toonie, sponge in hand. "I have all I can stand listening to that thing all day without having to look at it too. Clear it off. We've got work to do."

So Melba carried the guitar into the back

room and propped it carefully on Mr. Jiggs'
chair, where he'd be sure to see it first thing.
And though she didn't notice, every cat in the
store raised its ears to attention and watched
her go and come back. Then five of the big-
gest, including sad, three-legged Butch, padded softly out back and crouched near the
chair's legs, taking up a silent watch that
lasted for the rest of the morning. They left,
regretfully, only to respond to Miss Toonie's
low whistle. About noon, she decided that all
cats must be brushed and fluffed for their
grand appearance on Main Street.

"Can't have them looking like a bunch of
hoodlums," snorted Miss Toonie, brandish-
ing her hairbrush for the operation. And as
her own hair fuzzed and scraggled about like
a mad alley cat's, she went to work with
powerful strokes. But Melba saw that she was
careful to go gently, ever so gently, over all
the bruises and cuts and sore places that
might hurt a cat if brushed too roughly.

Chapter

—11—

IT TOOK MISS TOONIE TWO FULL HOURS TO BRUSH up the cats, what with chasing down the shy ones who slunk away to hide and fighting off the braver ones who wanted a second time through.

Meanwhile, Melba worked at the counter making signs on some dusty pieces of poster board she had found on a shelf. She found watercolor paints too, and brushes, and . . .

"The thing I like about plain old drug stores is they've got everything anybody ever needed," Melba told Miss Toonie as she rinsed off her brush between colors.

"Here Snowflake!" bawled Miss Toonie, groping under the candy rack. "Here Ozzie! Here Butch! Want a cherry?"

"They've got huge, modern drug stores in Glowville and Hopsburg, but no soda fountain to sit down at. They have aisles and aisles of things like popcorn poppers and dried flowers and giant boxes of washing detergent, but they never have what you really need. Like turtle food," said Melba, carefully painting a large red O.

"We've got turtle food," grunted Miss Toonie. She hauled Snowflake out by the tail.

"I know," said Melba. "I used to have a turtle. In Glowville you have to go to a special pet store to get turtle food. And you have to go to another special store to get your brother a jackknife for his birthday. And even another store to get the little bit of wrapping paper you need to wrap it up. At the huge drug stores all they have is huge rolls that cost five dollars each."

"We have jackknives *and* little bits of wrapping paper," announced Miss Toonie proudly. She held the poor, wriggling Snowflake by her scruff and fluffed up her tail.

"The Super Queen doesn't have a comic-book rack," Melba continued, "and it doesn't carry water pistols anymore."

"Probably why they're still in business and we're not," grumped Miss Toonie. "All these little things we've got don't make us any money." She looked at Melba sharply.

"How do you know what the Super Queen carries if you never go there?" she asked.

"Victor tells me." Melba shrugged. "The Super Queen isn't my kind of place."

Miss Toonie creaked up off the floor and brushed down her skirt, which was flecked with ten different colors of cat fur.

"If I may say so," she said, coming over to look at Melba's signs, "your kind of place is about to go out of business because nobody ever comes in it. So what are you going to do if this march works? If it works, we'll have customers jamming every corner and kids ordering hot fudge sundaes and all sorts of people you don't want to see!"

Melba gulped and turned to the old lady.

"But so will you!" she cried.

Miss Toonie stared at her. Then she glanced down at Melba's large, gay OPEN SUNDAYS sign, and at another one she'd painted further along the counter that said:

CATS MARCH FOR JIGGS'. INTRODUCTORY OF-
FER—ONE FREE ICE-CREAM CONE. COME 'N GET
IT!!!

"We should get started . . . if we're
going," said Miss Toonie.

"Are we going?" asked Melba.

Miss Toonie stared dismally at the signs.
And Melba, feeling her jitters stir around in
that deep place, wondered suddenly how
Victor's groundhog was getting along. He was
in a tight spot, all right. If he came up for
food he'd be shot, and if he didn't come up
he'd starve to death. Melba couldn't decide
what she would do if she were the
groundhog. She guessed the best way might
be to stay put in her hole and wait for the
hunters to go away. But knowing Victor, he'd
probably be up all night, so perhaps a dash
across the field for new territory would, after
all, be the better plan.

Miss Toonie had turned around to survey
the cats. All the brushing and fluffing had
stirred them up. Now they were swirling to
and fro across the floor, their groups massing
and breaking apart and remassing like rain
clouds on a windy day. They were edgy, un-
certain about what was coming next, and ir-

ritated that their old routines had been interrupted. Some streamed into the back room, thinking perhaps that Mr. Jiggs would suddenly appear there. They padded back out again to search the store with wide-open, worried eyes.

"Look at them," said Miss Toonie. "They know something is up and they don't like it."

"I don't either," said Melba.

"I don't either," sighed Miss Toonie, "but there's no helping that. One way or another this drug store isn't going to be the same comfortable, out-of-the-way place we've gotten used to."

"What if the Super Queen crowd starts coming here?" whispered Melba.

"I guess I'll be back to sponging off and worrying about clean spoons," groaned Miss Toonie.

They looked at each other nervously. Then, out of the blue, Miss Toonie snickered.

"Well! That's the limit!" she giggled. "Here we are scared to death of what will happen if the march works and scared of what will happen if it doesn't. Makes us sound about as spineless as Jiggs!"

Melba laughed, but not very heartily.

"I didn't like to say so, since I was the one who thought up this plan to begin with, but what scares me most is the marching itself. I never was very good at getting up in front of people."

"I'm not so hot in that department my-self," admitted Miss Toonie, "only I thought I wouldn't mention it and snarl the works. I've always been one for having a counter be-tween me and the rest of the world." She glared accusingly at the soda fountain counter.

"Listen," said Miss Toonie. "Just because we feel spineless doesn't mean we have to act that way."

"That's right!" declared Melba. Miss Toonie's confession about the counter made her feel braver.

"When it comes right down to it, you won't find *me* hiding behind the shades of some dark house!" bellowed Miss Toonie.

"Me either!" cried Melba.

"I guess nobody can take this drug store away from me if I don't want them to!" yelled Miss Toonie, springing into the midst of the swirling cats.

"Hooray!" screamed Melba. Miss Toonie put her fingers to her lips and blew the long, low whistle that shot every cat's tail straight up in the air.

"Come on, cats!" shouted Melba, and, a minute later, an impatient, if somewhat bedraggled line surged out the front door. At the head went Miss Toonie, in a coat whose pockets were temptingly stuffed with candy bars.

There was, however, one cat who, for reasons of his own, did not respond to Miss Toonie's hoot. While the other cats moved haltingly out to the sidewalk, Butch turned his old beaten body around and limped off into the back room. There he set up watch again under Mr. Jiggs' guitar, casting worried glances around the room.

Well, by now—maybe you've been noticing out of the corner of your eye—Melba has been sitting on the telephone for over an hour.

She has already talked to ten people at the *Guinness Book of World Records*. Five of them were secretaries who told her she had the wrong department. Three were switchboard operators who said the department she wanted was busy and did she wish to hold? (She certainly did!) The remaining two were line bargers who came on through a mistake in the connection and didn't know who they were supposed to be talking to either.

Melba, to kill time while she waits for the right department to show up, has been drawing pictures of the cats on her mother's doodle pad next to the phone. There's Butch about to crunch on another cherry. This one is Snowflake who, according to Melba, is so smart she's figured out how to open the cash register by leaning on the "sale" button with her paw. She likes the ring the register makes when she does it.

"But she won't do it if anyone is watching," says Melba now, cocking the phone's receiver on her shoulder in a professional way. "When anyone looks at her she acts stupid, like any dumb house cat in the world. A lot of Miss Toonie's cats are like that.

"We've got one cat called Fudge, on account of his chocolate color, who can answer the phone. Of course, he doesn't say anything after he's knocked it off the hook. He waits for Miss Toonie to pick up. Still, you've got to admit, it's pretty remarkable for a cat. But Fudge won't answer if you are watching him. He gets embarrassed and goes off to hide somewhere. He's afraid he couldn't do it if someone were looking, or that he'll be laughed at. I don't blame him at all. I used to feel that way.

"At school I was afraid to hold up my hand to answer a question, even when I knew the answer cold. I was afraid to walk across the room, even before Irma pinched me. When people looked at me, I felt as if a big, icy spotlight was shining down in my face, and I'd freeze. Victor said I made people nervous by freezing that way.

" 'Stay loose,' he told me. 'Nobody wants to talk to a frozen up person. It makes them feel frozen up too.'

"Stay loose. Stay loose. That's what I was saying to myself over and over as I started off on that cat march. I didn't think about how the cats were doing. I hardly noticed them. I suppose Snowflake and Fudge and all of them were shaking like leaves themselves (being out on that murderous street), but I was too busy worrying about whether I'd make it myself to pay attention to them.

"Shyness will do that to you," Melba explains. "You spend so much time thinking about yourself that you forget to think about other people. For instance, if I'd looked more closely, maybe I would have found out that a lot of other kids in my class at school were shy too. And afraid to raise their hands sometimes, and scared of Irma, which, I discovered later, nearly everybody was!

"If I hadn't had the spotlight in my face, maybe I would have noticed how the cats were becoming jumpier and more frightened with each block we marched; how their tails were curling down between their legs and their ears were flattening against their heads.

"Miss Toonie couldn't see it. She was walking on ahead. It wasn't her fault the cats went wild. I'm the one who could have stopped them but . . .

"Hush!" Melba interrupts herself. "Hello? Yes! This is Melba Morris calling about the dancing cats of Applesap!"

Chapter

—12—

BACK AT JIGGS' DRUG STORE, BUTCH CURLED his tail more tightly around his body. Otherwise, he remained motionless at the foot of the chair. Ten minutes passed. Then, about the time the grand cat march was passing through Applesap Center, causing the first townsfolk to blink their eyes, there came the sound of a key in the front lock. Mr. Jiggs, finding the door open, shuffled in and gazed dejectedly at the empty store.

"Cats?" said Mr. Jiggs in a low voice. There was no answer. He shuffled over to the soda fountain counter and peered behind it. Then he wiped his hand over the top of his bald head and went to the back room. As soon as he appeared, Butch got up and ran to rub himself fondly against the old man's worn trousers.

"Where is everyone?" asked Mr. Jiggs. He bent over to pick up Butch, who was showing no sign of the shyness Melba knew so well. Mr. Jiggs retrieved his guitar from the chair, and sat down heavily. He pulled a guitar string from his pocket and set to work replacing the broken string. Butch, perched on his lap, watched every movement with keen interest.

After a while, Mr. Jiggs spoke to Butch in the tones of someone long used to confiding in cats.

"They're up to something, aren't they, Miss Toonie and the others? And you don't like the looks of it. Well? Am I right? I appreciate your looking after my instrument all night. Do the same for you sometime."

The cat watched Mr. Jiggs closely.

"All that whispering by the soda fountain last night. There's a plan afoot, I don't doubt. Don't worry," added Mr. Jiggs dismally. "It won't come to anything. Nothing ever comes to anything these days."

He drew his thumb across the strings to test the new one for sound. It was flat. Slowly, patiently, he tuned the guitar until its old mournful chords rang harmoniously again. Butch's ears perked up. He leapt to the floor and stood eagerly looking up at the old man.

"Ah, old friend," sighed Mr. Jiggs. "What a time we had last night, eh? Never have I seen you cats perform so well. We've had some good parties in our day, yes we have." He strummed softly, and sadly.

"Having you cats about, well, it's been a pleasure, if I may say so. Never would have thought it. Never did like cats particularly. But then," he looked sympathetically at Butch, "I don't suppose you cats had much interest in music before we got together. We've made a strange mixture between us. Crazy, some would say." Mr. Jiggs stifled a giddy laugh. Then, as another thought struck him, he sat up and narrowed his eyes at Butch.

"Don't you ever," he began fiercely, "don't you ever *dare* tell Miss Toonie what's been going on these last few years. She doesn't like me. Never has. I couldn't stand the way she'd laugh and spread the news all over town: Jiggs has really lost his mind now, she'd say, playing orchestra to a bunch of loonie cats."

Mr. Jiggs' face flushed red with embarrassed anger. "And it wouldn't do you cats any good either. This is a private business between you and me. Don't want people stepping in and making a mess of it. I wouldn't trust them, not for a minute!" Mr. Jiggs slammed his fist against the strings, producing a harsh thump that flattened Butch's ears. But a moment later he relaxed.

"Well. Well," he said. "I'm sorry for how it must end. Still, store or no store, it couldn't last forever. I'm getting old." He wiped his hand over his head.

"I stumble and shuffle and forget things. Look how I forgot my guitar last night in the worry of saying our goodbyes." He shook his head gloomily at Butch, who stood rigid at his feet.

His words meant nothing to the cat. They washed through his head like an incomprehensible wind, sometimes fierce and frightening, sometimes low and soothing. It was the way of all humans—Butch knew from long experience—to speak and speak and at the end to have said nothing of importance. The old cat shifted his weight watchfully. He was waiting for Mr. Jiggs' voice to stop, and for that other language, the one he understood and craved, to begin.

He was waiting for the music, the fast, gay music that had become over the years, on lonely winter nights and parched summer evenings, through times of pain and times of suspicion, a way of talking between friends.

"We are here together," Mr. Jiggs' music said, appealing to all the cats, but especially to Butch, oldest and most deeply wounded. "Outside the world is strange and dark and trucks prowl the streets searching for us with their lights. Out there is uncertainty and danger. But here, while the sound lasts, we are sheltered. Here we can relax and be ourselves; act like cats, act like men, who cares," sang the music, "how we act. Let us dance because we are safe!"

Butch mewed a plaintive mew. But the old man's eyes were not on his guitar. They seemed to rest on something far off across the room. After a long time, he stirred.

"Come on," said Jiggs, getting up at last. Butch leapt for the door. "I'll sit out for a bit while you have a sniff around. It's not a bad day as days go."

Mr. Jiggs carried his chair out front, placed it in the open door to the shop and sat down again in the broad sunlight. There he strummed morosely while Butch nosed into the bushes. And there, a minute later, a piece of the day's sparkle caught onto his fingers. It caused a happy little tune to flare up. In a flash, Butch was at his feet.

"Hah!" cried Mr. Jiggs. "That was a pretty one! Well, I'll give you another seeing as there's something in the air that stirs it up."

Checking to see that no one was around to hear, he played another twinkling chord, and then a gay, strutting melody wholly unlike the mournful sounds Melba was used to hearing in the store. Then, feeling the music put cheer into his old bones, he let his fingers go and launched into a full-fledged song that danced up to the treetops and made the birds fall silent with admiration.

This was what Butch had been waiting for. In pure ecstasy, the old battered cat rose on his back feet, forgetting his injuries, forgetting that he was a cat at all and bound to obey the shy laws of catness. His head went back to face the sky. His tail curled and recurled around his body. His feet began a dreamy dance pattern that swirled him around, slowly at first, then ("Let us dance because we are safe!") faster and faster.

"Now you've got it, Butch!" roared Mr. Jiggs over the music, and neglecting all caution, he played on more loudly still, completely lost in his own performance.

He played so loudly, in fact, that he drowned out the sound of approaching footsteps, or, one should say, the drum of approaching paws. For at that moment, an unruly herd of ninety-nine cats was already turning down Dunn Street, thundering ecstatically toward the source of the gay talking music.

Chapter

—13—

IT WAS THREE O'CLOCK WHEN THE CATS SET off up Dunn Street, dutifully following Miss Toonie and the candy bars. Melba, taking up the rear, was talking to herself.

"Stay loose," she murmured through clenched teeth. She tried desperately to pretend she was Victor, but the jitters clutched at her throat. "Look straight ahead. Don't think who is watching. Stay loose. Stay loose!"

She was carrying the big sign CATS MARCH FOR JIGGS' nose high. Only her eyes and the top of her head showed above it. Around her the town breathed lazily and quietly and, suddenly (they were turning the corner onto Main Street), very strangely. Then it seemed to Melba not like Applesap at all, for all the houses were hunched together watching, and a queer wind blew, and there was a menacing straightness to Main Street that Melba had never noticed before. Before her the street stretched out like a narrow bridge slung between mountain peaks. Far below lay a treacherous valley floor. One false step and Melba would plunge over the edge. One false step and . . .

"ONWARD CATS!" screeched Miss Toonie from ahead. Melba jumped and pulled herself together. The line was approaching Applesap Center. By now, small knots of people were stopping to watch. And behind Melba, children on bicycles were catching up and keeping pace. They were laughing and calling. Melba held her sign higher and blushed. But, with the sign in the way, she couldn't see where she was going.

"Hey, you!" yelled a man's angry voice. "Get out of the road. You're blocking traffic!" A car horn roared in Melba's ear. She jumped back on the sidewalk. The cats were far ahead of her. When she ran to catch up, the bicycle riders (she was sure it was they and not the wind in her ears) snickered.

The marchers crossed School Street. Then Center Street. Then Melba's own Orchard Street, and here word of the parade seemed to have spread ahead because suddenly swarms of spectators were lining the streets, pointing and laughing. Melba was clinging to her sign as if it were a sinking life preserver when—

"Isn't that Melba Morris?" asked someone close by. "What does she think she's doing hiding behind that silly sign?"

Melba spun around in surprise. Irma Herring stood at the edge of her front yard amidst a group of girls, giggling. She was wearing a pale pink church dress, and pale pink ribbons in her hair. But self-conscious Melba, half blinded by sunlight and teetering again on the brink of that bridge, saw another color: Yellow! Immediately it seemed that she was back in her dream—the cat belly! yellow Irma!—and that the shooting must begin at any moment. Under Melba's feet the flat sidewalk trembled, and fell away.

Melba screamed. (This time it came out

loud and clear.) She dropped her sign and tripped over it. Then she too fell. And landed abruptly, scraping both knees hard on the pavement.

Irma doubled up with laughter.

"Why Melba Morris," she squealed with delight. "You're even funnier than these cats. I've never before seen so many dumb-looking animals all in one place!"

Maybe if Irma hadn't brought the cats into it, Melba would have gotten up and run away back to her room, crying. (Under the legs of her pants, her knees were bleeding.)

As it turned out though, Irma started crying herself exactly ten seconds after Melba hit the ground.

"Dumb-looking animals." The words streaked through Melba like a shotgun blast. They blew the dream away, and the bridge, and a second later they changed Irma from a frightening, gun-toting tyrant into the very same person Melba had been pinching, for months and months, up in her room.

Melba rose slowly, and walked over to Irma. She raised her hand. (Irma was still smirking.) Then she grabbed Irma's nose and pinched it as hard as she could.

Irma stopped smirking and screamed: "Let go!"

"No," said Melba.

"Help!" squeaked Irma. But no one helped. They stared. Irma pounded Melba with her fists.

"These cats are smart," said Melba quietly, but holding on tight. "They're smarter than you are."

"Okay! Okay!" shrieked Irma. She wrenched away and ran, sobbing, toward her house. Her friends hesitated, then followed her.

"I'm telling my mother about this," yelled Irma between sobs. "You'll be sorry!"

"No, I won't!" Melba called back. She dusted off her pants and turned to look triumphantly at all the people who, she thought, must have been watching.

But no one was watching. All heads were turned in the opposite direction down the street, where some sort of confusion seemed to have broken out: shouts and a bustle of movement. The crowd gave a collective gasp. Then, the cats hit.

They came thundering back down Main Street like a single, churning cyclone, tripping spectators and trampling Melba's sign to shreds. Children were toppled from their bicycles. Dried leaves and dust spun through the air.

"Mad cats! Look out!" people were yelling. They ran for cover as the herd charged through. Then shouting and pushing, they ran after the cats. Miss Toonie was in the middle flailing her arms and howling. But no amount of howling, or whistling, not even the candy bars which she waved in the air, could halt the cats' stampede. On they stormed toward Dunn Street, each cat nipping and hissing and scampering to be first. And on their tails came the frightened, hysterical crowds, and after them, Melba, running flat out.

Chapter
—14—

CATS ARE FAST RUNNERS. HOWEVER, THEY ARE not usually long-distance runners. Few animals can sprint up a tree faster than a cat, but when it comes to covering whole blocks at a time, most cats run out of breath or lose interest.

Miss Toonie's cats were five blocks from Jiggs' Drug Store when they heard the guitar music float past faintly on a wisp of wind. The speed with which they ran those blocks would have set a world record if anyone had been clocking time. Of course, world records of one sort or another are broken every day, only they mostly go unnoticed. Melba, for instance, had just broken two records herself that morning: (1) by being the first person ever to pinch Irma Herring's snooty nose, and (2) by being the first shy, ten-year-old girl to march down Main Street in a cat parade.

But Melba wasn't thinking about world records that morning, and neither were the cats, who came racing down Jiggs' front walk a solid five minutes ahead of the screaming crowd of spectators.

There, without even pausing to catch their breaths, they joined Butch at Mr. Jiggs' feet, and rose to dance. Butch turned his head to welcome his friends. From Mr. Jiggs there was no greeting. He was crouched over his instrument lost in his own wonderful music.

Never, it seemed to him, had he played so beautifully. His fingers, long accustomed to picking out tunes in gloomy indoor corners, took on a new quickness in the sun. The clear air that floated his melodies, also floated him, out of himself and away.

Not only was Mr. Jiggs unaware that the other cats had arrived. He did not hear the spectators who began to straggle up shortly after, gasping for air. They surrounded him in a wide, suspicious circle, and fell silent. First they stared at Mr. Jiggs. Then they stared at the cats, who were acting unlike any cats they had ever seen before.

As Mr. Jiggs trilled, one hundred mangy, beat-up felines swayed on their hind legs, lean and elegant and perfectly balanced. One hundred cat faces turned back to the sky in pure pleasure. One hundred cat tails curled and recurled rhythmically to the music, catching up and entwining each other, then weaving apart again.

"Gracious alive! They're bewitched!" gasped a woman.

But they were not bewitched, almost everyone could see that. The cats' dance was not weird or eerie. It was not a dark ritual left over from some unrecorded civilization. Neither did the cats appear hypnotized or crazed. They performed innocently and happily, like small children who, hearing the orchestra strike up at a party, dance out alone for the sheer pleasure of moving, unaware of how they may look, or of the grown-ups around them laughing and pointing.

"How beautiful!" gasped Melba. She had arrived almost in tears at the crowd's outer rim. Now she watched in fascination. The spectators were murmuring also. Some could not keep their own feet still, and swayed to the music's throb.

Then, too soon, the marvelous dance was over. Mr. Jiggs strummed a final chord. The cats came down daintily on all fours. The crowd shuffled and began to speak aloud.

Their voices brought Mr. Jiggs back to earth. Abruptly, his head shot up and he looked around, blinking heavily. Then before anyone could clap or race over to shake his hand ("What a tremendous performance!" people were saying), he leapt to his feet. Mr. Jiggs dropped his guitar with a clatter on the ground. His face turned a deep purple and his eyes bulged like marbles. He opened his mouth, and bellowed:

"Get out!" He clutched at the door with one hand. "Get away! All of you!" Astonished and hurt, the crowd stumbled backward.

"Go home!" shouted Mr. Jiggs, quivering with rage. He could have been yelling at a threatening pack of dogs. "You have no right here spying on me. Get out of my yard. Get away from my cats!"

A frightened child cried. People turned to flee. Here was the craziness they had expected to see after the wild chase down Main Street. Now the charm of the cats' dance went out of their heads, and was replaced by fear and anger.

Melba realized the danger at once.

"No!" she shouted, jumping to Mr. Jiggs' side. "No! Stay! This is a celebration! Free ice-cream cones for all and . . ."

"Get out," roared Mr. Jiggs, cutting her off. "We are closed. Go away and don't come back!" He picked up his guitar and stamped into the store.

So, the crowd went. Melba couldn't stop them. She tried, completely forgetting her shyness about speaking up. She pleaded and gestured and accosted everyone she knew by name. But nobody paid any attention, and Miss Toonie, who might have backed her up, was nowhere to be seen. One look at Mr. Jiggs, hunched over his wretched guitar, had been enough for her. One glance at the cats prancing eagerly at his spineless feet turned her heart to stone. Speechless with anger, she marched home, leaving Melba to face the furious throngs alone.

"Melba! Have you gone crazy? Do your parents know where you are?" barked a woman who was a friend of her mother.

"I'm going right home to phone the Glowville Humane Society," a man growled. "This town is infested with cats!"

Even the children went, called away by their parents. They mounted their bicycles and slowly pedaled off, glancing back over their shoulders.

When the people were all gone, only Melba stood, stricken, on the front walk. Around her cringed the cats, now frightened and disoriented.

"Poor things," whispered Melba, looking down at them. "It's all over for you now."

She opened the store's front door to let them slink inside. Then Melba herself went home, and the route she chose was an out-of-the-way one, and gradually, as she walked, her shoulders sagged and her eyes fell shyly down to her feet.

"It's a funny thing," said Victor that night, "but we didn't see a sign of that groundhog all day. He seems to have disappeared somewhere."

Even this news couldn't cheer Melba, who

crept away to her room, refusing to answer any of her parents' questions.

"A cat march?" said Melba's astounded father.

"Hush," said her mother. "Don't talk about it now."

Chapter

—15—

Now it would seem that jiggs' drug store was in a pretty hopeless position. Most would say, in fact, that it was in a worse position than if Melba and Miss Toonie had done nothing at all about the store's going broke.

For instance, if they had sat back and shyly twiddled their thumbs, nobody would have thought of calling the Glowville Humane Society to complain about the cats. Instead, the next morning, a large van pulled up outside the drug store and drove away shortly after with every one of Miss Toonie's friends packed inside.

Then again, Miss Toonie would never have been summoned to Hopsburg Civil Court and been fined five hundred dollars for obstructing traffic.

"And starting a riot in the peaceful town of Applesap, New York," declared the judge, shaking a finger at her.

"But your honor! I don't have five hundred dollars," cried Miss Toonie.

"Then borrow it," he answered curtly.

If Melba and Miss Toonie had followed Mr. Jiggs' example and moped in a corner, Melba's mother would never have received that angry telephone call from Irma Herring's mother.

"You must go and apologize to Irma," said Melba's mother.

For Melba, this was worse than Miss Toonie's five-hundred-dollar fine because it gave Irma the chance to snicker and tell everyone at school.

"That's what happens when you stick your neck out," Mr. Jiggs could have told them, but he wasn't talking to anyone. He was home alone behind his drawn shades, strumming his guitar.

Meanwhile, the store just sat there on

Dunn Street. No one moved out and, more importantly, no one moved in. The dry cleaning establishment had decided not to buy the place after all. They had heard about the grand march, you see, and didn't want a building where one hundred cats had been cooped up, going crazy, for heaven knows how long.

Of course, everybody had heard about the cats by this time. Even though they were over at the humane society now, people couldn't stop talking about them. People who had seen the cats dance told others who hadn't seen, and they in turn told more people. It became important in Applesap, and even in Glowville and Hopsburg, to know someone who had actually watched the dance in person. And if you happened to be a person who had been there, then that was even more important and you could feel very proud of yourself.

So, within a matter of days, the cat dance became a legend. The more people talked, the more extraordinary the cats became, and the more exquisite their dance, and the more unusual the whole event looked.

It wasn't long after that folks began to look at Melba as if she were some kind of wizard.

They stopped her on the street to ask questions. Curious children rode their bicycles slowly down the sidewalk in front of her house. Classmates who had hardly noticed that Melba was in their class turned around and stared at her sitting at her desk in the back of the room.

When people did those things, Melba acted the way she had always acted. She blushed, and stammered, and held her breath until they looked away. But, for once, nobody seemed to think this was stupid at all. Some people, she noticed, smiled at her timidly, as if they wanted to say something, but didn't quite dare.

One day, about a week after the cat march, Melba received a telephone call from the *Glowville City Crier.*

"The who?" asked Melba in alarm.

"You know. The newspaper!" hissed Victor, who had answered the call. "They want to talk to you." He held out the receiver to her impatiently, and with a look of long-suffering.

This past week had been an irritating one for Victor. At every turn—at school, at the Super Queen, in the street—he had been accosted by townsfolk whose curiosity revolved, in a most annoying and repetitive way, around a single point. That point was Jiggs' cat-ridden drug store, and by extension, his shy little sister's strange connection with it.

What was Melba up to? people asked. How had she gotten involved? Would the cats dance again? Was the drug store really closed?

"How should I know?" shouted Victor, in exasperation, because, more irritating still, he didn't know anything. Melba kept to her room. She wasn't talking.

"Am I supposed to be your press agent or something?" howled Victor through her closed door.

Now he held the receiver out to her as if it were yet another, deplorable insult.

Melba didn't like talking on the telephone any more than she liked going to parties. On the telephone, you had to talk fast, and clearly, and there was no time to think between words. People who talked to Melba on the phone nearly always ended by shouting at her: "Are you still there?" "Well, *say* something!"

"Come on. They're waiting," Victor said.

"But what will I say?"

"First find out what they want, dummy!"

Melba grasped the receiver as if it were Victor's shotgun, and said hello at about the same pitch a groundhog might have said it from a hiding place deep underground.

The voice that boomed out from the other end of the wire rocked her back on her heels. It belonged to Philip M. Riddle, editor-in-chief of the *Glowville City Crier*. Mr. Riddle was an impatient man with much on his mind. Foremost among his many worries was a dread fear of being beaten out for news by Hopsburg's competing newspaper, *The Howler*. Therefore, he came right to the point.

"Have they called?" he bellowed at Melba.

"Who?" she quavered.

Mr. Riddle took this answer to mean no.

"Well, thank heavens for that, anyway!" he continued. "We've been tracking this story like bloodhounds for two solid days, and, from what I hear, *The Howler* is doing the same. Whoever this Mr. Jackson Jiggs is, he's either never at home or not answering his phone. And this Angela Toonie, (you know her, I think) has had *her* telephone disconnected!" Mr. Riddle shouted in great disgust.

"Because of the five-hundred-dollar fine," Melba put in weakly. "She's broke." Mr. Riddle was unimpressed.

"So it's come down to you, young lady," he went on. "And what I want to know is, when can you stage it again?"

"Stage what again?" asked Melba, now feeling more amazed than frightened by Mr. Riddle's bellows.

"Why, the dance, of course! We've heard all about it. Everybody has. But a strange occurrence like that needs documentation. We want to run the story, but we'll need photos to prove that it happened, and since we weren't there the first time, naturally we'll need a restage job."

Mr. Riddle talked faster than anyone Melba had ever spoken to, on or off the phone. By the time she hung up, he had covered so much ground on so few breaths, that Melba was gasping herself.

"Whew!" she exclaimed, sitting back in her chair.

"What's up?" asked Victor. He had been slouching at the window, pretending an interest in the vegetable garden, where (further insult!) not a hair of any groundhog had been visible for over a week.

"Come on. Tell," he complained. Melba sprang to her feet and made for the front door.

"Great news!" she shouted. "I've got to go see Miss Toonie right away!"

A second later, she was gone. Victor shrugged. He picked up his shotgun and wandered out to the field to kick a few early-blooming daffodils.

Hold on a minute. What's all that noise? There is some sort of fight going on between Melba and the *Guinness Book of World Records!* Melba is yelling, and the *Guinness Book* is . . . is . . . Well, what is the *Guinness Book* saying? Are they coming to Applesap or not?

Now Melba has hung up the phone and flopped back in her chair, deep in thought. Her face has a beaten-up look on it.

"They say they're not coming," she answers at last.

What?

"They say they're not interested."

But that's impossible! These cats are fantastic. Who has ever heard of a shy, nervous animal like a cat getting up to dance right out in public? Who has ever heard of a hundred of them? It's a world record if there ever was one!

"I told them that," says Melba, shrugging. "I said our cats were an inspiration to the world and a lot more important than someone who swallows twenty-five nails.

"When you look at someone swallowing twenty-five nails, all you can think is: 'How terrible. Will he live through it?' But our cats, well, the way they dance makes people want to dance themselves. Their dancing makes you start thinking that maybe you can do things you never thought you'd be able to do. It's a miracle, but the sort of miracle that shows you what is possible."

And what did the *Guinness Book* have to say about that?

Melba frowns. "They wanted to know how old I was. And when I told them, 'ten,' they cleared their throats and said they'd put my report on file.

"And then I got mad and said age had nothing to do with the cats.

"And they said yes it did.

"And then I yelled that they'd be missing something if they didn't come look.

"And they said no they wouldn't.

"And then I said how would they like it if I called up 'Ripley's Believe It or Not,' instead.

"They said that was all right with them, and hung up in my face."

Poor Melba. That's the very thing she was afraid of. That's why she was nervous about calling them in the first place.

Melba shrugs again. "It's a funny thing,

but now that the *Guinness Book of World Records* has actually hung up in my face, it isn't so bad as I thought.

"In fact," says Melba, brightening up, "it's not bad at all!

"Hey!" she shouts, jumping up. "You know what? I'm not scared of them anymore! It's the same as when I pinched Irma Herring's nose. I didn't care what anyone thought about me, I just knew I had to do it. Only, with Irma, the feeling didn't last. I was back to getting the jitters the very next day.

"Now I think I'm on to something stronger," says Melba. "I guess it takes practice to figure out how to stand up for your rights.

"Do you know what I'm going to do now? I'm going to call the *Guinness Book of World Records* back. This time, I won't yell. I'll keep cool and keep on telling them why they should come out here and see the cats. And if they hang up again, I'll call them back. You just wait. This story's not over yet!"

Chapter
—16—

MISS TOONIE HAD NEVER BEEN A RICH WOMAN. She lived in a small, faded house on a seedy side-street in Applesap about twenty minutes walk from Jiggs' Drug Store. On her soda fountain salary, she had managed to furnish her home comfortably, if sparsely, with secondhand furniture. To save money, she did not own a car, or a television set, or a clothes washer. But she had enough to pay her heating bills and her electric bills and, if she was careful, a little left over every month to put toward her garden.

It was a small garden occupying a patch of

ground in front of the house. In part of it she grew vegetables, which, during the summer months, saved on her grocery bill. But the larger section, the section Miss Toonie scrimped for every year, was given to flowers, a wonderful assortment which she purchased as seedlings in May from a local garden shop.

Flowers pleased Miss Toonie. Usually, on a pleasant day this time of year, she could be seen out in her garden transplanting mounds of pink petunias, and white alyssum, and bright blue salvia from store-bought flats into the ground.

Now, however, Miss Toonie sat listlessly inside her house. There was no money for this year's flowers. The five-hundred-dollar fine had wiped out her savings and put her in debt. Occasionally, she rose to make herself a pot of tea, but even tea is expensive and soon . . .

But Miss Toonie was not thinking about money. She had made do on little and could make do on less. Flowers were a luxury. Cats, however, especially cats whom one had grown fond of, who were in all the world one's truest friends, were a necessity. Miss Toonie was lost without her cats. In the long week after the van had come to take them away (and how she howled against that! while spineless Jiggs merely turned his face away), in the long week afterwards, her face grew pale, the fuzz came out of her hair, her fierce, proud shoulders drooped and she walked like a slow old woman.

Minute by minute Miss Toonie thought only of her cats, and twice, in a fit of worry, she had visited by taxi their cages at the humane society. But to see them there, cooped up, frightened, rubbing forlornly against each other, had depressed her further.

"Well," sniffed Miss Toonie. "At least you have each other." Yet even this would not last, she knew. One hundred cats were too many for any humane society, even the most humane, to support for very long. There was the hope that a few of the least mangy and least broken-down might be picked out and taken to new homes. For the rest—no one wanted them, no one cared if they lived or died.

"Who else but me could love Butch's smashed face and awkward limp?" thought

Miss Toonie, gazing through the bars at her old friend. Given the choice between a dirty brown cat who can answer the telephone when no one is looking and a brand new cuddly kitten, which would a new owner select?

Miss Toonie came home, made another pot of tea, and sagged on her living room sofa. There Melba found her that afternoon, and it was a measure of Miss Toonie's utter dejection that she did not so much as raise her tired eyes when Melba told her about Mr. Riddle. Even when Melba told her about Mr. Riddle's promise to personally pick up the cats from the humane society and drive them to the — drug store for a morning of picture taking, she could not be roused.

"Useless. Useless," was all she said in a faint voice. "Jiggs would never agree."

"But, Miss Toonie! It could make the cats famous!"

"No, it couldn't. After the photographs are finished they'll be carted off back to prison again. People don't care about cats, never have and never will. Don't you start believing that one newspaper story can change that. I never believe anything I read in the papers, anyhow!" she added, getting up a bit of steam.

She slumped again. In the silence that followed, Melba lapsed into a fidget. Miss Toonie's limp misery was a strange thing to her, and Melba always grew nervous in the face of strangeness.

A knocking on the front door broke the silence. Miss Toonie tensed.

"Don't answer," she whispered. "I'm not seeing people." Melba sat still. The knock came again. Then, after a pause, a mournful call:

"Miss Toonie? I must see you, Miss Toonie."

Silence, while the old lady shook her head at Melba and Melba bit her lip.

"Miss Toonie!" came the cry again. The rapping was more insistent. "It's me. Jiggs. Open the door for heaven's sake!"

Melba sat up in surprise, and even Miss Toonie showed a bit of interest in this announcement.

"What does *he* want?" she hissed.

Melba shrugged in amazement. "Have you seen him since the march?"

"Of course not!" whispered Miss Toonie. "I figured he'd locked himself into his house for good. And well he might after what he did to my cats. Dancing after hours, what a thing!" she said bitterly. "Tell him to go away."

"Shouldn't you find out what he wants?" said Melba.

"Should I?"

"Yes. You should. Maybe he's decided to reopen the store."

"Hah!" snorted Miss Toonie. "He's deeper in debt than I am."

"Well?" said Melba.

"Well!" Miss Toonie spluttered and gave in. "All right then! Open the door and let the spineless fool in!" But she was drawing herself up on the sofa and smoothing her fuzz into place as Melba flung open the door and helped the yellow-faced Mr. Jiggs totter into the room.

Chapter

—17—

MR. JIGGS TOOK TWO WOBBLING STEPS INTO Miss Toonie's living room, and stopped.

"Is he here?" he gasped. "He must be here! I've been everywhere else!"

The old man was worn out. He clung to Melba's arm. But his eyes raced madly around the room and small drops of perspiration shone on his hairless forehead. Mr. Jiggs swayed to the right to peer into Miss Toonie's dim, lacy dining room. He veered left and looked up the steep stairway to the second floor. He staggered forward again, wiping his hand over the top of his head.

"Who?" Melba was crying.

"Who on earth?" Miss Toonie was calling out.

Mr. Jiggs was too distraught to answer directly.

"The back porch," he panted. "Where is the back porch?"

"I don't have a back porch," snapped Miss Toonie, losing her patience. "And will you kindly tell me who it is you are barging about my house looking for?"

Mr. Jiggs wilted, and dropped into a chair by the front door. But he sat forward a second later, beckoning to Melba.

"Go look," he wheezed and pointed, "at the back yard. Some door or other. Some window. I saw him, you know. Nearly had him. And he was sitting on my back porch!"

"Who!" shrieked Melba and Miss Toonie together in final desperation.

"Butch, you fools!" roared Mr. Jiggs. "Who else?"

He wilted again, and laid his head against the back of the chair, and closed his eyes.

Miss Toonie shook her head.

"See?" she muttered at Melba. "He's gone crazy. I told you not to let him in."

But Melba was watching the old man closely. How small he looked, flung back in the chair. And his face, she noticed, was not red or purple or bulging, but white. It was white and very frightened.

"Mr. Jiggs?" she asked gently. "What has happened to Butch?"

"He's gone," came the answer. "Escaped!"

"When?"

"Early this afternoon." Mr. Jiggs opened his eyes. "I nearly had him," he moaned again. "But he couldn't wait. He saw them coming after him."

"Who?" said Melba. Miss Toonie knew the answer to that. She was already on her feet.

"The humane society," whispered Mr. Jiggs. He glanced over his shoulder. "They are searching the neighborhoods around Glowville and Applesap. And they have made radio broadcasts. I've heard them myself. Rabid, they say he is. Crazed. Dangerous!" He turned and appealed to Miss Toonie.

"He isn't, you know. He just wanted to get out."

Without a word, Miss Toonie wheeled and ran for the windows on the far side of the house.

"He's hurt," Mr. Jiggs called after her. "Cut. The barbed wire!"

"I can't see him," Miss Toonie shouted back. "I'm going out to call." A door banged shut.

"Barbed wire!" cried Melba. "What happened?"

Mr. Jiggs insisted on getting up again. He positioned himself by the living room's front windows and, like a fearful sentry, peered around the edge of the curtain at the street.

"I heard a noise—a sort of cry—from my back porch," he began, "and when I lifted the shade to see what it could be, there was Butch! Well, it wasn't the first time, of course. He knew my house. He used to come sometimes from the store to find me late at night. Then we'd keep each other company. But this time, I couldn't believe my eyes. I'd seen him not an hour before at the pound, you see, cooped up with all the others."

"Butch came to visit *you?*" interrupted Melba in amazement. Mr. Jiggs shrugged. His pale face reddened.

"And you went to see the cats?" Melba persisted.

"Of course I went!" Mr. Jiggs flung the

curtain aside and looked far off down the street. "I couldn't leave the cats there to rot by themselves. I went every morning," he said, turning to glare at Melba. "And what's wrong with that?"

"Nothing!" cried Melba. "Only we thought you didn't care. Miss Toonie said you . . ."

"Miss Toonie! What does Miss Toonie know!" Mr. Jiggs choked and swung back to the window. *She* didn't see me. I saw her, though, moping in front of the cages. I wasn't about to let her see me!"

"But why?" asked Melba, thinking suddenly that this was the first conversation she had ever had with Mr. Jiggs. Poor old fellow. He looked beaten down in a new way now; a new, terrified, cornered way.

He was wearing a lumpy, gray raincoat much too large for his small frame. It made Melba think again of what a fragile old man he really was. His roarings and bellowings were not so very frightening when you looked closely. He used them, thought Melba, like the raincoat itself, as a rather flimsy cover against a lifetime of bad weather and worse luck; against disappointment and self-disgust and people who had once expected great things from him (Druggist of the Year, perhaps!), but who now, like Miss Toonie, only shrugged and frowned when his name was mentioned.

Poor lonely man. Melba felt sorry for him. He had not one friend to stand by his side: not a grumpy Miss Toonie; not even a brother who was a wild man. He was too embarrassed to allow himself any friends.

"Never mind why," Melba said quietly. "What about Butch?"

Mr. Jiggs swung around again and fixed her with a fierce eye.

"Well, as I was saying, I saw Butch. But before I could get to him, he ran off. Then I saw a black humane society van coming down the street, and I was beginning to put two and two together when the telephone rang. Without thinking, I answered. It was the humane society calling to report Butch's escape. They thought he might turn up at the store, and wanted to warn me. Hah!" Mr. Jiggs face puffed with anger.

"Butch had jumped an employee, a woman who was walking the cats in an outdoor pen, they said. He leapt on her, and from her onto a fence. And he clawed his way up and escaped through barbed wire over the top. They know he was cut because of the blood. And the woman is scratched. She is hysterical. She thinks Butch is rabid. Only a rabid animal would act in such a crazy way, she said. Only a sick cat would rake itself through barbed wire and run to get away!

"But don't you see?" shouted Mr. Jiggs. "He'd had enough. Miserable cat! I've had the feeling myself!" He was shaking with anger now and Melba found herself stepping away from him. After all, there was nothing flimsy about Mr. Jiggs' rages. They were ugly and menacing, a threat to everyone within earshot. Melba was backing slowly into the kitchen when a door banged again. Miss Toonie shot into the room.

"Butch is not here," she announced. "But the humane society is!"

Melba and Mr. Jiggs spun around to the windows, and gasped. Outside, a little way off, a black van was moving cautiously down the street. A man was walking beside it, keeping pace. He stopped to examine a back yard, and when he stopped, so did the van. And then together they proceeded on again.

The man was wearing heavy leather boots. In his hand he carried a stick.

The van came abreast of Miss Toonie's house, and now Melba could see the gold letters painted on the side: Glowville Humane Society. The van stopped. A door opened and a second man stepped out, a big man in identical leather boots who gestured and called the first man over. They met on the sidewalk and spoke to each other. But their eyes, as they talked, were probing the bushes in Miss Toonie's front yard, and the ragged weeds in her flower bed, and finally, the steps of her front porch.

It was as the three inside the house watched this scene with wide-open eyes, and strained to overhear the conversation, that another noise suddenly caught their ears.

"Meow," came the noise, soft and shy.

"Mew," from somewhere out back.

"Meow,"—let me in—Butch was calling.

Chapter
—18—

LATER, MISS TOONIE WAS ABLE TO RECON-struct Butch's flight: how he had instinctively chosen the only road that might take him direct from Glowville to Applesap; how he had arrived at the drug store (bleeding badly, the signs were there on the front step) and prowled around its shuttered windows in vain; how he had sought out Mr. Jiggs' house, where, sighted by the black wheeled monster that dogged his heels, he had bolted into brush, and dragged himself through back yards, in a direction he vaguely sensed might lead to Miss Toonie.

("But how did he know?" Melba was to ask, many times, in the weeks following. "He'd never been to Miss Toonie's house!"

"Blind luck," was Victor's answer.

"Humph!" said Miss Toonie. "You can think that if you want!")

Later Miss Toonie explained everything, but now—now Butch lay on the kitchen floor with a gaping wound running down his left side. It shocked them all to see it.

"Towels!" bellowed Miss Toonie. "In the linen closet, top of the stairs!"

Mr. Jiggs raced for them.

"Antiseptic!" he roared down.

"In the bathroom cabinet! Get the cotton, too!"

"Hot water!" they cried, converging again in the kitchen while, in the middle of their rushing, Melba knelt at Butch's head and stroked the sad, beaten-up face. It was streaked with mud. Burrs snagged in the fur. Butch's one eye was open. It seemed sleepy and distant. Melba stroked softly and tried to whisper comforting words.

"You're home, old cat," she told him. "Don't worry. You're home and nothing can happen to you now."

But even as she spoke a loud knock sounded at the front door. And Miss Toonie, at work cleaning the wound with a piece of cotton, heard it. And Mr. Jiggs, turning up the stove under a pan of hot water, heard it. And they all froze.

"The humane society!" breathed Mr. Jiggs. No one could think of what to do next. They stared at each other. They stared at Butch, lying torn and bleeding between them. No one could think of anything at all.

"They've seen him," croaked Miss Toonie. "They know he's here!"

Panic, like a cold icy light, spread over the kitchen, and, as if it had been struck by a fairy tale curse, the little group turned to stone. Time passed. The knock came again, harder this time.

Perhaps from long experience, Melba was the first to move. After all, she'd had some practice dealing with icy spotlights and turning to stone. Jitters—and they were thick in the room at that moment—were things she battled daily. But jitters were usually frightened feelings that Melba had about just herself. Now, she was frightened for Butch, who lay bleeding to death at her feet, and for Miss

Toonie, who loved him, and for Mr. Jiggs, speechless with terror.

Perhaps it was being frightened for everybody that gave Melba the courage to move. Perhaps it was forgetting about herself.

Melba stood up and, out of habit, adjusted her glasses.

"Miss Toonie," she said softly, "you hide Butch. Carry him somewhere. Anywhere. Mr. Jiggs will bring the towels and cotton.

"Quick!" she added, for they were slow getting started. "Take him to the cellar. I'll handle the humane society. I'll tell them you're not here."

"They won't believe you," groaned Miss Toonie. "Oh, what shall we do? What shall we do?"

"Yes, they will believe me," whispered Melba, "if I do it right. I've got an idea. I think I can manage." And suddenly, she knew she could manage. Her mind was clear, and cool, and very, very smart.

"Go on," whispered Melba, as another loud knock rattled the door.

A minute later, Melba was opening it timidly. And smiling politely. And rubbing her skinny elbow—she knew just how to do

that—in such a way that anybody looking at her would know she was a shy little girl who was afraid to answer questions. Anyone who looked would see in a minute that she was scared to death of her own voice; too scared to be much help in finding a crazed, rabid cat; too shy to tell anyone anything but the absolute truth.

"Nobody is here," murmured Melba to the two giant men who stood on the front porch in their creaking leather boots. "And I haven't seen any cats today."

The leather boots were suspicious. Hadn't a frightened neighbor just reported seeing a large gray cat in this very back yard? Hadn't the men themselves watched someone—an older woman perhaps?—open a window and scoop something—perhaps that very cat!—off a ledge? Wasn't this Miss Toonie's house, and she a known lover of cats?

Was she? Had they seen that? Melba rubbed her elbow harder and looked confused. But underneath the tortoise-shell glasses sliding crookedly on her nose, her mind sped smoothly down a single track.

"Oh! It was me you saw," she answered meekly. "I wasn't scooping anything. Just cleaning the house and shaking out a dust rag. Miss Toonie isn't here. She went to look for the cat."

The men shrugged at each other. They scuffed their boots on the ground and looked over her shoulder into the living room.

Wasn't anyone else here at all?

Melba shook her head.

Was Melba absolutely sure she hadn't seen that cat?

Melba was sure. She was so timidly sure, and so seemingly terrified by the thought of a rabid cat on the loose, that the men began to feel embarrassed.

"Didn't mean to upset you. Nothing to worry about!" announced the man with the stick.

"You stay in the house," added the other. "There's no way to tell what a crazy cat like that will do next."

Melba nodded, and twisted her fingers into a fantastic knot. Behind her glasses, her eyes narrowed slyly. Her plan was working!

The man with the stick caught the look. Instantly he was suspicious again. He beamed his eyes on Melba's face like a bright light, and for a moment Melba thought he was looking straight through her. Straight through into the cellar below, where three forms huddled in the darkness, listening, and trembling, and fearing the worst.

But who could be suspicious of Melba's small, shy head bent over that extraordinary snarl of fingers? The man dropped his eyes and turned to go.

"Take care," advised his friend. They walked back to the van and continued along the street, moving slowly, terribly slowly, so slowly that it seemed to Melba an hour passed before she dared fling open the cellar door and call triumphantly down to those hiding in the gloom.

Chapter
—19—

"LIGHTS!" CRIED MISS TOONIE. MELBA flicked the switch at the top of the stairs. Mr. Jiggs' pale face looked out from behind the furnace.

"Gone?"

"Gone!" yelled Melba. "I did it! I *did it!*"

There was a scuffling and a scraping behind the furnace. Then Mr. Jiggs was lumbering up the stairs with an energy Melba had never seen in him before. And he was shaking her hand, and bellowing like an ecstatic bull: "Brilliant work! Splendid job! Miserable cellar! We thought you'd never come!"

He flung himself back down to Miss Toonie, helping her to her feet and propelling her across the floor. Butch lay cradled, amidst towels, in her arms.

"Stop pushing! You'll squash the poor

cat," she snapped. Mr. Jiggs, however, was not to be contained. He leaped and fluttered about her, and when she stumbled mounting the stairs would have picked her up and carried her, Butch and all, if she hadn't kept him at bay with one elbow.

"Look what she's done! Made a bandage out of cotton, and in the dark too! He's stopped bleeding!" crowed Mr. Jiggs. He pumped Melba's hand again and pranced out to the living room windows to inspect the street himself.

"How is Butch?" Melba asked Miss Toonie as she lowered the cat gently onto the kitchen table.

"He'll be all right," she answered sternly, "if that old fool will stop shouting."

But even through her sternness, she looked pleased and couldn't help giving Melba a bony hug. Melba blushed and grinned with pride.

"It's about time a plan of mine worked."

"We couldn't imagine what you were doing up there," said Miss Toonie, smiling. "Jiggs was sure they had dragged you kicking and screaming off to jail. He was really quite worried. We couldn't hear a thing, you see!"

Melba grinned again. "I was being shy," she said breezily. "It comes in handy sometimes." Then, from the living room, Mr. Jiggs exploded with an enormous sneeze that made them both jump, and laugh.

"He's allergic to cellar dust," Miss Toonie confided. "We had to stop him up with towels while you were handling the humane society. I've never seen a man so terrified to sneeze. I think he would have strangled himself rather than give us all away." The old lady seemed unaccountably cheerful over this report. And when Mr. Jiggs appeared in the door threatening another gigantic explosion, she handed him her own handkerchief before pushing him off into the living room. He backed away, shamefaced, and erupted violently up the front stairs.

Butch needed more attention then, and more towels and more cotton were hauled down from upstairs. The wound was properly cleaned, and a real bandage devised, of adhesive tape and sterile pads, by Miss Toonie. She'd had a good deal of experience at such things and knew just what to do. Finally, the old cat was settled in a cozy nest on the living room sofa. Mr. Jiggs sat beside him, ruffling his ears and admiring the results of Miss Toonie's nursing. Miss Toonie sank back in an arm chair and drank a cup of tea, while Melba curled up cross-legged on the floor.

"Now! Tell us how you got rid of the leather boots," begged Miss Toonie. So Melba did, and between them all an easy conversation flowed, with much chuckling and joking.

Mr. Jiggs told about a particularly terrible sneeze that he had avoided in the cellar by crossing his eyes and blowing out his ears. This made them laugh so hard that Butch woke up and had to be lulled back to sleep with more pats and rufflings.

A peaceful silence followed. Miss Toonie gazed fondly at the cat. Then, she turned her eyes on Mr. Jiggs.

"Dancing indeed!" Melba heard her mutter. "You might have told me, you know. It wasn't as if I went home to a roaring fire and family dinner every night."

Mr. Jiggs glanced up at her. "I thought you would laugh," he answered humbly. "And I couldn't have anyone spoiling things between me and the cats." He looked down at the bandage. "You fed them and petted them and talked to them all day long. But at night, the cats were mine. We took a long time to get to know each other. But when we did, well . . . we had some grand times together."

Mr. Jiggs sighed. "The cats were all I had, crazy or not. I didn't want anyone taking them away from me."

"Well, they've been taken away now, all right!" sniffed Miss Toonie.

"Yes. All but one, anyhow. We'll keep Butch, of course. We couldn't get on without him, I can see that now. Neither of us."

"But that is not good enough!" cried Miss Toonie. She sat forward in her chair and, catching Melba's eye, gave her a slow cat's wink. Melba grinned and winked back. Miss Toonie cleared her throat.

"Now listen here," she told Mr. Jiggs. "What would you say if I asked to see the cats dance again? Just once more, for old times. I didn't get a proper view the first time, anyway."

Mr. Jiggs hesitated. He rubbed his hand over the top of his head. He ruffled Butch's ears.

"But how?" he said at last. "They're in the pound?"

"Not how, but when!" Miss Toonie struggled to her feet. "And I think tomorrow would do very well." She turned to Melba for confirmation. "Tomorrow then? And to top it all off, we'll have Mr. Riddle's *Glowville City Crier* over for a look, too!"

Mr. Jiggs sat straight up on the sofa.

"What?" he shrieked.

"Hooray!" shouted Melba.

Chapter
—20—

How it was that every person in applesap, and most of Glowville and Hopsburg as well, had heard about the cat dance restaging job by seven o'clock the next morning, no one could ever say.

It wasn't from Miss Toonie. She sat up all night making tea and talking Mr. Jiggs into a performance he didn't want to make.

It wasn't from Melba, who ran home to call Mr. Riddle on the spot. She told only Victor and her parents about the dance. Not that she wouldn't have dared to call up someone, and tell him, by now. After dispatching the leather boots and telephoning Mr. Riddle, she felt capable of practically anything. She just didn't know anyone to call yet.

The news didn't come from Mr. Riddle. He spent his evening hounding the Glowville Humane Society, whose officials were doubtful at best about the idea of releasing ninety-nine cats into his care.

Victor may have called a friend or two, and told them to bring along some cherry bombs to liven things up a bit, but that didn't add up to the crowds that began arriving, shortly after dawn, on the sidewalk in front of Jiggs' Drug Store.

Somehow, from sources unknown, by a sort of osmosis perhaps, everyone for miles around had got wind of the news. And that night they talked about the news, and went to sleep and dreamed about the news. And the next morning they leapt from their beds and trampled down their doors to be the first out to see the news in person. No one was going to miss out on seeing the cats dance this time. No one wanted to wait around for Aunt Millie to call to tell them they should have been there.

It didn't matter that the day was a plain,

old midweek Wednesday, with work to be done and schools to be attended. No one even bothered to proclaim a holiday. They simply came, men, women, and children, and stood on the sidewalk. And their cars clogged the Applesap streets bumper to bumper so that the mayor himself couldn't get his own car out of the driveway. He had to huff all the way to the store on foot.

By the time he arrived at eight o'clock, Miss Toonie had opened up and was selling hot coffee by the ton to anyone who could get close enough to the counter to grab a cup. The store was jammed, and the front steps were jammed, and the sidewalk seethed and swarmed with craning necks.

People from Hopsburg were stumbling over people from Glowville and striking up conversations. Strange Glowvillers were button-holing strange Applesappers and deferring to their opinion of what, exactly, the correct time was. And Applesap folk, pleased as peacocks to be visited on home ground, were pointing out the beauties of Applesap (even if it didn't have a roller-rink pavilion) and loudly proclaiming the advantages of shy, quiet towns.

Victor was there talking guns and escaped groundhogs. Irma Herring was there terrorizing her friends with smart remarks. The woman who thought the cats bewitched was there waiting to see if they would be bewitched again. Even the man who had called the humane society to complain about cat infestation in the first place was there, peering down the street and wondering when on earth the celebrities would arrive.

Melba was there, of course. She was helping Miss Toonie pour coffee and selling candy bars to the kids. Every five minutes she scooted into the back room to check on Mr. Jiggs. He was nervously tuning his guitar, and breaking strings, and predicting wholesale rout and ruination.

"Are they here?"

"Not yet."

"Are they here now?"

"Not yet."

"Are they now?"

They came at last. At a little past nine o'clock, a howl went up from the crowd as a black van edged to the curb and stopped. Mr. Riddle stepped out, triumphantly appraised the size of his audience, and walked around to open the back doors. The cats emerged. The spectators surged. The cats spat and bolted. The spectators roared and pushed. Then, there was chaos.

APPLESAP CATS DANCE BEFORE CHEERING THRONGS! was the banner headline across the front page of the *Glowville City Crier* that afternoon. But, whether the throngs had actually cheered, or had been shoving and pummeling and shrieking at each other, was a matter for interpretation. As for dancing, there was doubt in the minds of a few as to whether the cats had performed at all. Somewhere in the mob, Mr. Jiggs had, presumably, played his guitar. Somewhere in the fray, a few cats may have risen to stagger briefly on their hind legs. People claimed to have seen them. Photos accompanying the news story seemed to show something of the kind.

It was difficult, of course, looking at the photos, to tell precisely which blurry body might be cat, and which human. But the spirit of the event was there in a tangle of black and white. And the throngs were pleased to pieces to have been present on the spot. They went home to buy newspapers and to clip stories—

stories to send their friends, and to stick on their bulletin boards, and to carry in their wallets, and to preserve and frame and read to their children's children.

"A thing like that doesn't happen every day," they advised each other, which was wrong, of course. It could have happened every day and might have if Mr. Jiggs hadn't brought his fist down on the soda fountain counter and said once a week on Saturdays was certainly enough. The performance had aged him and the cats fifty years, he growled.

"Don't be so bossy," snapped Miss Toonie. "It's not as if I like parading the cats out in public. I don't. It goes against my grain. This is for the good of all of us, and the store. We've got to get business moving again!"

"Business IS moving!" roared Mr. Jiggs, waving his arm around the store. "Look at it!"

Business was moving, all right. The morning after the restaging spectacle, it had arrived with a clatter of feet at the store's front door, pushed its way in, stayed all day, and complained about being put out at night. A week later, the shelves were emptying at such an alarming rate that Miss Toonie doubled up on her orders for everything. The next week, she tripled. The next week, well, by then it was obvious that once a week was quite often enough for the cats to dance. People came by in droves no matter what day it was. They came to stare at the cats, who were getting used to being stared at and beginning to feel rather proud of themselves. They came to stare at Miss Toonie and Melba and Mr. Jiggs. They stayed to buy. And to eat: hot fudge sundaes, chicken salad sandwiches, cherry sodas, scrambled eggs. Miss Toonie was learning to cook all over again. After school, Melba ran the cash register before the admiring eyes of the Super Queen crowd. They were 'the Jiggs' Drug Store crowd now, a polite and friendly bunch who overlooked such minor details as spotty spoons and crusty counters.

"And they're ever so much easier to talk to!" exclaimed Melba.

On Saturdays, though, there was no time to talk. Saturdays, the store turned into a one-room carnival.

"We ought to start taking reservations by phone," snorted Mr. Jiggs. "Either that or ask

for police protection. The cats and I were nearly trampled to death last week."

He pretended to be as fiercely gloomy as usual. But underneath lurked a happy man, a proud and satisfied man who needed only more practice at success to become a thoroughly pleasant human being.

For Mr. Jiggs had found, after the initial jolt, that he liked performing publicly. He was good at it, he discovered. He liked making money, too, and beating out the Super Queen for customers. And he liked, especially, the new, respectful way Miss Toonie looked at him when he came to work each morning. Why, Miss Toonie was a changed woman, Mr. Jiggs announced. She bid him good morning every morning and good night every night, and she made suggestions for running the store that proved to be extremely helpful.

No longer did Mr. Jiggs cower in the dismal back room. He strode about in the open now, and took charge of matters that hadn't interested him in years. He fixed the leaks, and ordered air conditioning, and made plans for expanding into the lot next door. The cats needed a dormitory of their own, he said, a place where they could be housed and fed and nursed in comfortable surroundings.

"Befitting their noble talents!" declared Miss Toonie, whose respect almost hit the ceiling at this announcement, and had to be held down with a long series of unconvincing sniffs.

"To get them out from underfoot!" grumbled the old man.

The cats, of course, had moved back into the store the very day of Mr. Riddle's restaging riot. The humane society was testy about it at first. But after they found out that only over Miss Toonie's dead body, and Mr. Jiggs' and Melba's dead bodies as well, would the cats return to Glowville, they decided to head home alone.

"Do you really mean it about the dormitory?" Melba asked Mr. Jiggs. "Won't it cost a great deal of money?"

"We'll get striped red awnings for the windows, too," he answered, trying to smother a smile. "We've got to smarten up if we're to be a national landmark."

"Who said anything about national landmarks," sniffed Miss Toonie, who was still trying to recover herself. "You're turning my cats into a three-ring circus."

"Our cats, you mean," retorted Mr. Jiggs. "And there's another thing. We're hiring a publicity agent. People are calling and writing from all over the state of New York to find out about this store and how to get here. We need someone to handle them."

"Publicity agent, my foot!" shrieked Miss Toonie. "Melba's been handling those people for weeks, and helping me behind the counter too!"

"That's right," said Mr. Jiggs. "And now she's hired."

"Hooray. Hooray! *Hooray!*"

That's Melba in the living room, isn't it?

"They're coming. They're *coming!*"

Look at her. She's jumping up and down like some groundhog who's just found a brand new, unguarded, vegetable garden way across town. Her glasses are falling off her nose. Her hair is a mess. Now she's doing a hot shuffle and snapping her fingers, as if she were someone in the movies who'd fallen in love on Fifth Avenue.

It's a good thing Irma Herring isn't here to see this. She'd laugh her head off.

"Who cares!" screams Melba. "They're coming! Next week. Next Saturday, to be exact. The *Guinness Book of World Records* is coming to Applesap, New York. Can you believe it?

"It was a snap!" she yells, snapping her fingers once more. "This time I didn't let them make me wait around for the right department. I asked for the editor-in-chief straight out. I must have sounded impressive because I got him almost immediately. 'Why haven't I been informed about these cats before!' he demanded. He said he might come to see them himself."

Melba hoorays some more, spins around twice, and sits down suddenly in her chair. Now, she is trying to look calm and collected, the way a publicity agent should look in a situation like this. But how should a publicity agent look? Who knows? Who cares! Melba is up and dancing again, and she's not at all worried that someone might be watching.

"I've given up worrying about that," she announces. "I took a lesson from the cats. You should come over to Jiggs' Drug Store and watch them now. They don't have to wait for Mr. Jiggs to play his guitar before they get up and dance. Of course, they still perform on Saturdays—that's their big event—but even on off hours they'll jump up and start twirling. Miss Toonie says they've turned into a bunch of showoffs and she doesn't like the looks of it one bit.

"I like it though. I *love* it. When you think of how those cats used to look, beaten-up and cringing, and how they look now, fat and proud of themselves, you can't help but think that showing off is what they need to do most. I guess I've been doing some showing off myself. Victor says he doesn't like to come down to Jiggs' to watch the cats dance anymore because he has to watch me too, strutting around talking to people and boasting about the cats.

" 'That's what you do all the time!' I told him. 'Only you boast about rabbits and groundhogs and shooting up the town.' He didn't think much of that. Wait until I tell him about the *Guinness Book!* I bet even Victor would have been afraid to call them up on the phone the way I did.

"Speaking of which," says Melba, plunging into the kitchen. "I'm going down to the drug store right now to tell Miss Toonie and Mr. Jiggs the news. Why don't you come with me? You'll get to see Miss Toonie sniff and tell me I'm turning the cats into a three-ring circus. And you'll get to see Mr. Jiggs forget about being gloomy for a minute so he can run over and shake my hand. And you'll meet Butch. He still isn't up to dancing because of his wound. Miss Toonie keeps him behind the counter with her, where he can listen to Mr. Jiggs' guitar without getting stepped on. He's a strange old cat, quieter and shyer than the others, and, if you ask me, he's not ever going to be a public performer. Maybe it's because he's been beaten up once too often. Maybe it's because he was born shy and would have been shy no matter what. It's hard to tell."

Melba stops a minute and takes off her glasses to polish them thoughtfully on the edge of her jacket.

"There's one thing about Butch, though," she adds, "and you've got to admire it. He may act shy on the outside sometimes, but inside, when he comes right down to it, he knows he can stand up for himself. Just because he's shy doesn't mean he'll let people walk all over him. No, sir," says Melba.

"No, sir!" she yells, heading out the door. "Come on. I'll show you what I mean!" Then off she marches, with a kind of swagger in her step. It might make people think (those who happened to be looking out their windows right then) that Melba Morris was getting too big for her britches. She is, in fact, and she's not the only one.

These days, a lot of people in Applesap are outgrowing those small, timid britches they used to wear in the shadow of those louder and pushier towns of Hopsburg and

Glowville. They're exchanging them for a larger size: the right size for being a national landmark seven days a week and a one-room carnival on Saturdays; the right size for being listed in the *Guinness Book of World Records;* the perfect size for a roller-rink pavilion to beat the devil out of Glowville's and Hopsburg's.

"The main thing," shouts Melba from halfway down the block, "is to tell people how to get here. See, all you do is take a pin, or a thumbtack, or a jackknife and stick it, pow, in the very middle of the map of New York State. That's where Applesap is, at dead center. You can't miss it!"

ABOUT THE AUTHOR

JANET TAYLOR LISLE grew up in Connecticut and has worked as a newspaper reporter and freelance writer in Georgia and New York. A graduate of Smith College, she lives now in Montclair, New Jersey, with her husband and daughter. *The Dancing Cats of Applesap* is her first book.

ABOUT THE ILLUSTRATOR

JOELLE SHEFTS was born in San Antonio, Texas. She graduated from Pratt Institute with a degree in Fine Arts, and is a filmmaker as well as illustrator. *Blue Collar Capitalism*, her latest film, has been shown nationally on PBS, on German television, and was given a special showing at the Museum of Modern Art in New York City. She lives in New York with her husband and young daughter.